STRIPPED DOWN

By Mae Harden

For my sister, who pushed me when I needed it and my husband, who is now required to read a romance book.

Chapter 1: Olive

As I shepherd my friend's bridesmaids back into our hotel, I can't help but smile. This has been one of the best, most ridiculous, nights of my life. Sure, maybe sweet, innocent, virgin Chelsea should have stopped and thought about it before letting our friend (and resident wild lady) Sally plan her bachelorette activities. We've suffered no shortage of girly drinks, carousing, and penis jokes.

When we get to Chelsea's room, Sally slips into the bathroom and reappears with two bottles of champagne. I don't even know where she had those hidden. Just because she's creeping up on 65 doesn't mean Sally has settled down one bit. With her curly riot of lavender hair and a leopard print pantsuit, she led us on a bar crawl of downtown Napa. Each stop featured a different sexual cocktail along with a gift for each of us, tailor made to make Chelsea blush as hard as possible.

I met Chelsea in high school during the two torturous weeks I spent on the track team, and she's been my bestie ever since. When she asked me to be a bridesmaid, I jumped at the chance to be part of her big day. Though, I never could have predicted that a bachelorette party for someone like Chelsea would reach such epically filthy proportions.

We started with Pink Silk Panties in the hotel suite where we opened little gift bags containing pale pink thongs. The color is demure but the barely there polka dot mesh screams "Watch me strip." I'm pretty sure Chelsea's soon to be husband will pant like a dog if he catches her wearing it. Next was a round of sweet-as-shit Bend Over Shirleys and bottles of strawberry flavored lube. Chelsea blushed as pink as her drink and asked what you use flavored lube for.

Then there were the Leg Spreaders with a pair of fluffy handcuffs, the Screaming Orgasms with high-end vibrators. The Pop My Cherry shots with a full set of white bridal lingerie from Sally's boutique, complete with a little veil on the back of the white cage panties for Chelsea. The rest of us got black lingerie minus the veil. I started pumping the breaks and passing half of each drink back to the bartenders. Sugar and alcohol don't love me as much as I love them so I switch to seltzer with lime early on.

Poor Chelsea has been a flustered mess all night, Googling how to use each gift before squeaking and throwing her phone back in her purse. I've never had so much fun. Chelsea's twin cousins from Boston, Kate and Kristen, started out the night as buttoned-up as her, but with each of the dirty drinks, they loosened up a little more. The bartender at our last stop was an excellent sport, but once they started calling for more "shawts" while modeling their lingerie over their clothes I knew it was time to go. They had one too many Slippery Nipples, and it was starting to show.

It's only 12:30 when we get back to the hotel room, but the party isn't even close to over because Sally puts on some classic rock while waving her pink panties in the air. God, I hope I still party like that in my 60s. Kate is dancing on the couch but Kristen looks like she's wilting and I ask Sally if we should put her to bed.

"Don't you dare! She'll miss the entertainment!" Sally hoots over the music. Oh no. I've been friends with Sally long enough to know this can't be good.

"What entertainment?" Chelsea asks innocently.

Oh, sweet baby girl… I think to myself. "Sally, tell me you didn't." She smirks and straightens the jacket of her pantsuit.

"What kind of bachelorette party doesn't have a hunky stripper?" She looks like the cat that ate the canary.

"The nice kind," I reply. Poor Chelsea's eyes are round as saucers and she's gone pale. "The kind of bachelorette parties for virgin brides!" I hiss at Sally.

"She won't be a virgin after Christmas!" Kate crows from her dancing platform on the couch. Chelsea blushes so hard I'm worried she will burn up. Her Christmas Eve blowout of a wedding is fast approaching along with the inevitable end to her virginity.

Kate and Sally clink glasses and chug the remains, letting out another "Woooo!" I can't help laughing. I've never been a woo-girl but when Chelsea puts on a brave face and follows suit, pounding the last inch of her champagne I can't help but join in. It's her night.

Sally squints at the clock, "What time is it?" She asks.

"Almost 1:15."

"Damn stripper is late!" She scowls as she tries to pop another bottle of champagne, holding it between her thighs in the least ladylike display I have ever seen. There's a pounding on the door and her head whips up, lips lifting in an evil grin.

"Open up ladies! You're being too damn loud!" The voice filtering through the door is a deep baritone and one of the sexiest things I've ever heard. The festivities have gotten to me because I've never gotten so turned on by a man's voice before.

I give Sally the evil eye as I open the door. "I can't believe you ordered a strip... Oh my fucking god." The sight in front of me sends a shiver through my body.

This man is not at all what I would have expected from a stripper. I guess I was expecting a cheesy, oiled up, twenty-year-old that man-scapes and thinks he's Magic Mike incarnate. This man must be in his late 30s with a short, well-kept beard and chocolate brown hair. There's a sprinkling of silver-gray hairs at his temples. Fuck me. Why is that so hot? He's rugged and muscular in a way that makes me think he works with his hands.

His flannel has several buttons undone at the top, showing off the broad expanse of his chest, dusted with dark brown hair. My eyes drift down to his jeans, slung low on his hips and the muscular V that dips into the waistband. I know I shouldn't look, but I can't help myself because either he's stuffed a sock down his pants or that bulge promises a lot. I can't swallow because my tongue seems to have grown too big for my mouth.

Sexy Lumberjack leans an arm against the door frame and looks me up and down, his deep blue eyes sweeping over me, burning me. Jesus, how much did I have to drink? I'm turning to a puddle under his piercing gaze. A very wet, hot puddle. I'd love nothing more than to run my hands over his bare chest. I want it so badly my fingers are twitching and I curl my hands into fists to stop myself.

"You ordered a stripper?" he asks. He's still wearing a steely expression, but there's a hint of a smile underneath it.

"Nuh… nah…" Holy shit, I can't talk. "You don't look like a stripper..." I start but then I throw a hand over my mouth. Was that rude? "Sorry, I didn't mean that. I mean, you look like you could strip. Obviously you've got the body for it... I just thought strippers would have less chest hair…" Oh fuck my life. Why did I just comment on his chest hair?! I sound like a babbling idiot.

Sally saves me, calling out from somewhere behind me.

"That was me, sugar. I booked the stripper."

Sexy Lumberjack takes his eyes off me for the first time since I opened the door and smirks. "Is it just the five of you? I expected at least a dozen ladies dancing on tables from all the noise you were making."

Sally pouts. "I ordered a cop, not a cowboy. You don't even have a hat."

He chuckles, "I'm not a cowboy, I'm a contractor."

"Close enough, I guess." Sally shrugs and reaches around me, grabbing hold of a muscular arm. He lets her pull him into the room, watching me as he slides past. His body so close to mine that his bare chest rasps against the front of my dress, making my nipples pebble. It's all I can do to keep my drunk self from licking him. Drunk Me is a horny mess.

Sally jumps on the couch in her heels. "Let's see it, Mr. Contractor!" I am one hundred percent sure she will be paying damages to the hotel.

Mr. Contractor just looks at us like we're crazy. This must be his first time because he looks like he has no clue what he's doing. What the fuck is going on? I mean, I've never actually seen a stripper, male or otherwise, but aren't they supposed to come in with a boom box and props and stuff? Despite being the sexiest man I've ever laid eyes on, this guy doesn't seem prepared. Those jeans don't even look like rip-aways.

"I just came over because you're all being so loud…"

"Hurry up and strip so we can put Kristen to bed!" Kate calls out.

He cocks an eyebrow and gives us a stern look. God, that shouldn't turn me on.

Chapter 2: Brooks

I wonder if I should just strip for them. I'm not particularly shy about my body. I might not be stripper-level ripped, or even a good dancer, but I could fake it for a couple minutes and then maybe then they'll settle down and go the fuck to sleep. I must be truly desperate to get some peace and quiet, or I would never consider this.

The frisky lady in the leopard-print suit hoots at me and selects a song on her phone. Familiar lyrics followed by an iconic BWOW WOW. The unmistakable first beats of You Give Love a Bad Name blasts out of the in-room sound system. I rub my hand down my face.

"Bon Jovi? Really?"

Leopard-print Lady starts a chorus of WOOs but the stunning woman still standing by the door doesn't join in. Instead, she watches me with a distrustful, almost appraising expression on her face. Like she can't figure me out.

She seems less drunk than the rest of the party, which isn't saying much, but she's not jumping on the couch or wearing her underwear over her dress. Her sexy curves and bright green eyes are shown off to perfection in her little blue dress. Long black hair falls in soft, touchable curls. My hands flex, dying to get tangled up in it.

She's not just pretty. She's fucking beautiful, but more than that, something in her eyes has my cock stirring in my pants. I've never felt drawn to a woman like this. I feel like I need her even though, logically, I know I can't have her. She's just passing through.

"Yeah, sorry ladies. I'm not a strip--"

"TAKE IT OFF! TAKE IT OFF!" Chants the brunette wearing a lacy bra on top of her dress. Green Eyes cocks an eyebrow. One part challenge and one part curiosity. I can tell she wouldn't mind if I lost a few pieces of clothing.

A frustrated growl rips its way out of my body. Fine. Whatever. I just want them to go to bed so I can sleep. I'll never see any of them again anyway, right? They'll be leaving and heading back to wherever they came from. Boston, if the accents are anything to go on.

The woman in the bride sash throws her hands over her eyes, but I'm not worried about her. I lock eyes with the woman by the door as I unbutton the rest of my shirt. Her pretty mouth hangs open as she watches me. I can think of a dozen dirty and obscene things to do with that mouth. Her gaze slides down my bare chest, lower, lower, lower... So I pop the button on my jeans and kick my boots off. I'll do this all night if she's the one watching me.

Chapter 3: Olive

If this man is a stripper, I'll eat my baker's hat. Don't get me wrong, I'm not complaining. He doesn't even glance at Chelsea, despite her hot pink BRIDE sash. Instead, he pins me in place with just a look as he undoes his shirt. His eyes rake over my body, leaving hot trails of awareness everywhere his gaze lingers.

His shirt hangs open and maybe I'm shallow, but dear god his abs are giving me the dirtiest fantasies. Is licking a stripper inappropriate? If he even is a stripper, that is. I'm pretty sure strippers are supposed to dance. He isn't dancing, but this is so much better. This feels... intimate. This feels like it's just for me. The other girls are only getting to watch because they happened to be here.

He slides the shirt down his shoulders and tosses it right at me. I catch it on pure instinct because the logical, thinking part of my brain has completely failed me. Shamelessly, I bring his shirt to my face and breathe it in. It smells like lumber and pine and fresh laundry. Oh jeez. Of course he smells like heaven. It's not enough that he looks like a god. Maybe he'll toss me the pants next...

As if he can read my mind he flips the button on his jeans and lowers his zipper. I can see the top of his black boxers in the open V of his pants but instead of losing the pants he shoves a hand down the front of his underwear and gives himself two long, slow strokes. Oh god, I think I'm drooling. Did I just moan out loud?

Just as quickly as it started, the song is over. The other women sit silently, watching with gaping mouths as Mr. Contractor removes his hand from his pants and zips them back up. He doesn't bother with the button before stalking towards me. "Go to bed, ladies," he growls. His eyes never leave mine and I'm frozen to the spot, just drunk enough that common sense has abandoned me.

Sally pops up from her spot on the couch where she's been fanning herself. "Hey! I paid for the full hour!"

"And I told you, I'm just a contractor that needs you ladies to be quiet so I can get some sleep. You're welcome, by the way," he tosses over his shoulder. He stops in front of me and he's so close I can barely breathe without my chest touching his.

My back is against the wall, giving me no place to go. The warmth radiating off his body sets my heart pounding at a frantic pace. I'm still clutching his shirt to my face, covering my mouth and nose as if I can hide from him.

He looks at me hard and arrogant for several seconds. Long enough that I squirm under his ominous glare. It's almost like he's angry at himself for liking what he sees. Or maybe he's angry because I clearly like what I see. I don't care. Either way, my skin is tingling and aching for him to touch me.

"Go to bed." His voice rumbles through my body as he pulls his shirt from my grasp.

I don't enjoy being bossed around. I would also be lying if I said I didn't want to see how this fuck-hot man would react if I push back, so I lift my chin. "Make me."

He gives me a threatening look, one that might make a lesser woman give in. Not me. "Maybe I need a goodnight kiss first," I say tauntingly as I rest my hands on his chest. I can't help but notice the way his hard pectorals flex under my finger tips, their raw power barely contained.

"Ah, fuck it," he husks. His hands catch my wrists, pinning them to the wall beside my head as his lips crash down on me, his body pressing mine into the wall. The world could burn down around me and I wouldn't care because, right now, this man is the only thing that matters. The hard planes of his body grinding against my curves, his dominating mouth claiming me, and the deep groan of lust that rumbles out of him.

My body gives into his, melting like chocolate on a sultry day. I'm putty in his hands. He tears his mouth from mine, releases my wrists, and with an intensity that sends shivers skittering through my body he whispers, "Go to bed."

Chapter 4: Brooks

I can't believe I just did that.

I figured my buddy Sheldon was doing me a favor when he offered to let me stay in one of his unbooked hotel suites while my floors were being resealed. He was even thoughtful enough to warn me there was a bachelorette party booked next door and they might get "a little rowdy."

I just didn't expect the walls to be so thin or the party in question to have a marathon weekend of siren impersonations. Or the green-eyed beauty with a smart mouth. I always liked a mouthy woman. The kind of woman who wouldn't take any of my shit.

It's been way too long since I've had a woman pressed up against me and that wasn't just any woman. Groaning, I think about the way she tasted. The way she writhed against me, so close I could feel the heat of her pussy through her dress. Gritting my teeth, I roll over in bed. The bachelorette party has finally gone quiet. I'd give anything for them to carry on and give me an excuse to go back over there. I'd like nothing more than to lay claim to the green-eyed woman.

She deserves better than a cold workaholic like me though. Running a construction firm is demanding. I have funneled every ounce of my time and energy into my company for the last nine years. It's taken a shit load of planning and hard work, but there's a reason my reputation is one of the best in Napa. And it's not because I go around kissing random chicks.

I toss and turn for hours, waking up over and over to thoughts of the green-eyed woman who is sleeping less than 50 feet from me. I could probably yell through the wall, and she'd hear me. Sleep doesn't take me until I decide to find out who she is first thing tomorrow morning.

When I wake up, I'm still exhausted. I groggily fumble for my phone only to realize I slept through my god damn alarm and I'm late to my initial job site. I'm forced to rush out of the hotel at record speed and pray the bachelorette party is staying one more night.

I curse myself the entire drive out to the site. I should have at least asked for her name and phone number last night. My inner caveman would have been happier if I had thrown her over my shoulder and carried her back to my room. Instead, I just stalked out and spent a sleepless night alone, wondering where she lives and who she might go home to. The thought of another man kissing that pouty mouth, putting his hands on her body, has me grinding my teeth.

I struggle through the first few hours of my day. I need more coffee and I can't shake the need to find her. I'm tempted to cancel my client meeting in Sonoma and drive around Napa to see if I can spot the bachelorette party. I didn't even want to take the damn meeting in the first place. Commercial additions aren't our usual business but I owe Della, the architect, a favor, and the bakery owner is a friend of hers. If I cancel now, she will be royally pissed.

The drive up to my client meeting in Sonoma only takes 20 minutes and I'm early. Parking in front of the Olive Branch Bakery, I check the lot for Della's car. It looks like I beat her here so I look up the number for the hotel and call the front desk, asking to be connected to room 613. The phone rings and for a second I panic, because I don't have a plan of attack for this. I'm usually methodical to a fault, but this girl has me all messed up. It doesn't matter because the phone rings and rings and rings some more. They've either still asleep, gone out for brunch, or they've checked out.

I call the front desk again. When the desk attendant answers I go with a white lie and my friendliest voice. "Hi, my fiancé is in room 613 and no one is answering the phone. Could I leave a message for her?"

I can hear a keyboard clicking as the desk attendant looks something up. "I'm sorry sir, we don't have any guests registered to that room. What is your fiancé's name?"

Shit. "Oh, she's calling me on the other line," I lie. "Thanks for your help!" I hang up and stare at my phone for a couple of seconds before tossing it in the passenger seat. "Dammit," I mutter through clenched teeth. Sagging in my seat, I ponder my options. The sign in the bakery window catches my eye, announcing that they sell locally roasted coffee. At least I can take care of one of my problems before this damn meeting.

Chapter 5: Olive

Holy shit."

"That's what I said!"

"He kissed you and stormed out, naked, into the hotel hallway?" Lilah, my sister asks with a wide smile.

"Well, not naked. He was wearing his pants." My heart pounds a little at the memory. I try to channel the emotion into the enormous batch of brioche I'm kneading.

Lilah snorts, "And a massive boner, most likely." She's scooping muffin batter into the tin in front of her.

"Yeah, it was just about at full salute." I laugh a little, but it's bittersweet. By the time we got up this morning, the maid was cleaning the suite next to ours and I realized that I have no idea who our mystery stripper was. I guess it doesn't matter. If he had wanted to get in touch with me, he would have figured it out. I'm just going to chalk it up to the crazy peak of a wild night. Sigh.

"That was one hell of a longing sigh, Olive. Was it really that good of a kiss?"

Before I can answer her, my head baker, Luis, joins us back in the kitchen.

"How was your lunch?" I ask him.

"Who kissed you?" Luis asks, his brows lowered with concern. I smile at him affectionately. If any man had the right to worry about me, it's him. Luis has been a father figure for us ever since Dad left us with Gran. We practically grew up with his two sons, Marcos and Javier.

His wife died a couple years back and even though he could have retired, he insisted he would be bored and lonely. So, when I opened my bakery two years ago, Luis was all too happy to come to bake with me. I don't think we could function without him. He bakes the best bread of anyone I know. Because of his fresh rolls and bread, we sell tons of baked goods to the local restaurants; he's helped make us the most successful bakery in Sonoma.

"A stripper kissed her!" Lilah giggles with so much evil glee that I'm wondering if we should perform an exorcism.

Luis looks aghast. "Olive!"

"Oh my god. He wasn't really a stripper." I try to wave Luis down as I explain. "He was just this random guy in the hotel room next to our party... he only stripped because Sally begged him." I grimace because somehow that sounds worse.

Luis is far from placated. I can see him spooling up for a lecture on safety but I'm saved by a "Yoo-hoo!" from the small hallway that leads to the dining area. Della's blonde head peeks around the corner. "You ready to talk construction?"

"Hey lady! Give me a second." I wave at her and slap the dough in front of me.

Luis takes over the brioche with a disapproving eyebrow for my late-night antics, but he keeps his mouth shut. For now, at least.

"Thanks," I tell him, popping a quick kiss on his cheek. He sends me on my way, muttering under his breath about making smart choices.

I join Della by the hand sink, hanging my apron and hat on their hooks. "Sorry to keep you waiting," I say to Della as I wash my hands. She's all smiles today, caffeinated and ready to talk shop.

"No worries! I can't wait to get your classroom finished. I've been trying to figure out how to make macarons like yours for years. You have to promise you'll teach me when the addition is done." She rubs her hands together with glee. "I drew up some preliminary sketches I want to go over with you and the contractor. You are going to love this guy. He's a total pro. Best in the area." She grins widely and holds her hand up like she's telling me a secret. "He's not too hard on the eyes either." Della's a lovable weirdo and a talented architect. I'd hire her even if she wasn't giving me the Friends and Family discount.

Lilah joins us, hanging her apron and hat next to mine. She's promised to help me teach some classes and I want her involved in the planning process as much as possible. She splits her time between baking here with me and tending bar over at Blue Ruin Speakeasy. I'd like her to partner with me full time, but I think she likes bartending too much to give it up.

Following Della out into the dining area, I start to ask her how her husband is doing, but one glance at our new contractor stops me in my tracks. The man sitting at the table in front of me, sipping coffee from one of my mugs is one I'll never forget. His stormy blue eyes look over the edge of the cup and he chokes on his coffee, sputtering, "Holy…"

"Shit." It's not ladylike, but it's the only thing my brain can spit out. My entire body is frozen, but my ability to swear seems to be intact. Out of the corner of my eye, Della is shooting looks back and forth between me and the gorgeous man at the table.

After a beat, Lilah busts out into cackling laughter. "No! Oh my god, Olive, no. Tell me this isn't the guy." She's laughing so hard she's wheezing between sentences.

The man sitting in front of us collects himself faster than I do. He stands, and he's even taller than I remember him being last night. Although I guess I'm in kitchen shoes, not three-inch heels like the last time I saw him. His bearded jaw is clenched, muscles visibly straining. He keeps a straight face as he holds out a hand to shake mine.

"Brooks Davidson. You must be Olive."

Chapter 6: Brooks

Fuck-fuck-FUCK. She's here. How is she here?! This cannot be fucking happening. Olive Donovan isn't just my afternoon appointment. She's the woman I stripped for and kissed against a hotel wall last night.

I was already trying to figure out how to get Sheldon to break hotel confidentiality and give me the registration info for the party. I'd even contemplated how hard it would be to break into his office and look it up as a last resort. I guess I don't have to bother now because she's not only a local, she's my god damn client.

I've never crossed the line with a client before, but here we are. Client or not, I know I'm going to cross that line again. Maybe I should be worried about my company or my reputation, but as soon as I left the hotel room last night I regretted leaving her behind.

Olive looks just as shocked to see me as I am to see her. Her mouth is hanging open, her eyes round as she stares at me as if she's afraid I'll do another striptease.

She's wearing a clean, white chef coat over tight black pants. Gone are the sky-high heels, tight blue dress, and smokey eye makeup. She is fresh-faced, her long hair tied back in a ponytail, and somehow she's even sexier like this. I'd like to take her ponytail and wrap it around my fist while she... I'm going to halt that train of thought before it can leave the station.

Della's eyes are bouncing back and forth between us, confused, and the girl behind her is cackling. I can only assume that Olive told her what happened last night.

I'm fighting back the urge to kiss her again. Hauling her into the nearest closet to see if she tastes as good as I remember sounds like a great idea right now. If I could just get her somewhere private... Jesus, I need to get control of myself. Somehow I keep a straight face as I hold my hand out to Olive, introducing myself as professionally as possible. I don't know how to fix this but maybe I can salvage something from this mess.

Olive Donovan seems less than happy to see me. She stares at my outstretched hand like it might bite her. She finally reaches out and shakes my hand quickly before trying to pull free. I grip her small, warm hand and I hold my breath for a second, trying to quell the excitement coursing through my body.

"It's really nice to meet you," I say.

Her green eyes flash at mine with heat and anger. Her pretty mouth tightening into a scowl. "Oh, yeah. Super nice to meet you," her voice dripping with sarcasm. Well, crap. She's pissed, and even her anger is charming. I bite back a smile that will probably just piss her off more.

While I refuse to give Olive back her hand, Della recovers her composure and springs into action, grabbing the giggling woman by the elbow and leading her away. "Lilah, why don't you show me the kitchen."

As soon as they're out of earshot Olive hisses, "What the hell are you doing here?"

She doesn't pull her hand back again. In fact, she squeezes mine harder as if she's trying to be threatening. I try to contain my smirk but don't do it very well. "I told you I was a contractor, sweetheart."

"Don't call me that," she hisses. "Did you know who I was last night? Because this is fucking embarrassing." Using the hand I'm still gripping, I pull her closer. I want to hold her curvy little body tight against mine, but this probably isn't the place.

"How would I have known who you are? And why are you embarrassed? It's not like you did anything." Her gaze softens and zeroes in on my mouth while I'm talking. I'd bet anything she's remembering exactly what she did. Taunting me to kiss her and the way she kissed me back. Melted for me, rubbing that sexy body up against mine.

The sight of her little pink tongue wetting her lips sets my body to aching, and it's everything I can do to contain the groan wanting to escape my chest. Trying, and failing, to muster a scrap of self-control, I step closer, letting the scent of her vanilla and sugar skin wash over me.

"I'm the one who should be embarrassed. I figured you were from out of town and it wouldn't matter if I made an ass of myself. I didn't know you were a client. If I had known, I never would have laid a finger on you."

The soft look vanishes, and she yanks her hand out of mine. "Jesus, you really know how to make a girl feel special." Her eyes turn hard, and I realize too late that I've insulted her. Possibly hurt her. "Let's just focus on what we have to do here, ok?"

"Olive, wait--"

" I hope you're a better contractor than you are a stripper," she says.

I narrow my eyes at her. "It was a mistake, but I'll remind you that you *did* ask me to kiss you. Practically dared me."

Her face colors. "Wow. It's fine. It never happened. Napa might not be Vegas, but last night can sure as fuck stay there." She turns on her heel and strides back to the kitchen. "Let's go, Mr. Davidson."

Chapter 7: Olive

Wow. What. An. Ass. Seriously? His big excuse is that he thought I was from out of town and he'd never have to see me again? Sure, why not just pin a woman to the wall and kiss her as long as there are no consequences? And then he says I dared him to do it? Douche.

I can't believe how much time and energy I've wasted thinking about that kiss. I didn't expect to see him again but I genuinely thought he was attracted to me. I guess I was just the chick closest to the door. He never would have kissed me if I hadn't pushed him. Dared him. Whatever. I've never been one to push myself where I'm not wanted. I'd rather be alone. I can totally pretend the kiss never happened.

Sure. And somehow I'll just ignore the way my skin tingles with awareness when he's close to me.

Stalking back into the kitchen with Brooks behind me, I catch Della and Lilah whispering with Luis. All three of them snap their mouths shut, guilt written all over their faces.

"You three done gossiping? Can we get to work?" I head out the side door of the kitchen and breath in the crisp dry air. December in Wine Country is peaceful. It's chilly enough that I should have grabbed a sweater to throw over my chef coat, but I can deal for a couple minutes. I actually welcome the cold. Maybe it will cool me off.

I've wanted to add a classroom to the bakery since I bought the building, but getting the main bakery financially successful had to come first. We've been in the black for a couple of years and this last summer was so profitable that getting the loan for my addition was a piece of cake, considering how much we can charge for classes and parties in the extra space.

I even have the perfect space for the addition. The bakery's building is a large L shape, with a gravel lot in the corner of the L. Right now, we use the space to hold dumpsters and for overflow parking. We have plenty of parking without this space though, and we can move the dumpsters easily enough. I can already see what the addition will look like in my mind.

I walk Della around and give her an idea of how I want to arrange the classroom. I already gave her a sketch of the layout so we can plan the electrical and ventilation. She walks around the space taking notes and measurements, conferring with Brooks on materials. I'm careful to avoid making eye contact with him, but it's hard to miss the way he looks at me. I struggle to push away the memory of last night every time I feel his eyes on me. And as much as I'd like to, I can't ignore his voice as it rumbles over me, talking about lumber and timelines. Stupid sexy voice.

My sister stands off to the side adding a little something here or there, but mostly she watches my refusal to look at Brooks and sends lots of questioning looks my way. I try to give her my best stop-looking-at-me-like-that face, but she's having too much fun with my suffering.

Della claps her hands and tucks her metal clipboard under her arm. "All right! I think I've got everything I need for now. I'll get back to you with plans and once we confirm everything, Brooks can get you the estimate. Easy peasy."

I meet Brooks' eyes, but his face is unreadable. Della, sensing trouble between me and the contractor, pulls me aside, a warm arm hooked in mine. "You okay, sweetie?"

I pause, thinking for a second. I don't want her to think I'm unhappy with her or ungrateful. She's an amazing architect and I'm lucky she offered to do my addition and gave me a ridiculously generous discount. "I know you will do an awesome job. I'm not worried about you at all... but why this guy?"

Della purses her lips and whispers, "Look, Lilah filled me in. Maybe I shouldn't have let her, but I'm nosy and I love gossip. Not one of my best traits, I know. Despite the... weirdness from last night, Brooks is an amazing contractor. He's one of the very best in the area and he's available to start right away. He always finishes his jobs on time and on budget. If you want to go with another contractor, I can find one, but they probably won't be able to start right away. You risk not having the bakery ready for tourist season. That would suck, right?"

Ugh, okay. Fine. "Yes, that would really suck."

"Great!" Della is back at full volume again. "Let's go inside where it's warm and sign some paperwork!" God, she's so chipper. I hate her a little right now. Following her back inside, she moans as the bakery air hits her. "What are you guys baking? It smells like heaven."

"It's the lemon poppyseed cake. I've got it in muffin form up front. Let me grab you a couple," I offer, watching out of the corner of my eye as Brooks motions for Della to lead the way back to the table. I don't miss the way he watches me as I split off and head behind the counter.

My barista sets up a French Press for me while I go to the pastry case to grab the muffins. My hand hovers near them, but I don't pick them up right away. I can see Brooks through the glass sitting at the table with Della. The vindictive side of me is tempted to only grab two and let Brooks go hungry. But I'm not that person, and I have to work with him for the next few months. Oh, god. Months. This is going to be so unpleasant.

I tamp down the urge to be petty and plate three muffins, setting them on a tray with the coffee, three mugs, and some half and half. When I look up, Brooks has his eyes glued on me again. Heat shoots through my body. My stupid body has gone rogue and doesn't give a rat's ass that he doesn't want me.

My body doesn't at all care that he only kissed me because I taunted him and he wanted to shut me up. But reminding myself that he considers it a mistake, one he never expected to have to face again, is enough to throw a cold wet blanket on my hormones.

Chapter 8: Brooks

The only way this day could have gone any worse would be if Olive had refused to work with me. Until she signs the paperwork, it's still a genuine possibility. It's obvious she's pissed at me, but it's not like I said anything that wasn't true.

When Olive joins us at the table I'm surprised to see that she brought me a muffin and a cup of coffee. When I meet her eyes and thank her, all I get in return is an icy stare and a small nod. I feel a twinge of guilt. I don't like seeing her so angry at me.

Olive sits between us at the small square table. When she sits her knee brushes against mine and she flinches, honest to god, flinches before turning her body towards Della to avoid touching me. Jesus, I don't know what nerve I hit with her but it must have been a fucking doozie.

The only upside to the way Olive has positioned herself is that I can watch her while Della walks her through the timeline for the planning phase of her addition. She's so expressive. I can see each thought as it passes across her face. I'm captivated by the delicate arch of her eyebrows, the way her long lashes flutter as her eyes narrow and holy hell, the way she moistens her lips with the tip of her tongue.

I watch her lift her coffee cup to her lips and I'm oddly fascinated by her wrists. They look so tiny and fragile sticking out the end of her chef coat. I have a flashback to the way I grabbed them and used them to hold her against the wall last night. It's a miracle I didn't bruise her. Fuck. She's so small and vulnerable. The thought of another man, anyone at all, grabbing her like I did, has me clenching my jaw. Fuck that, I decide as I grind my teeth. She's mine and I'm going to fucking protect her. No one is getting their hands on her but me.

Subtle I'm not. Della catches me watching Olive and her eyes flash with a warning before asking me to walk Olive through the construction timeline. I do my best to keep it professional, but she won't meet my eyes.

I'm still trying to figure out how to get Olive to warm back up to me, when Della stands, interrupting my thoughts. "Well, I think that's everything. I know Brooks has other clients to meet and you have delicious things to bake so we'll get out of your hair. I'll be in touch soon, Olive."

They hug and Olive offers her some cookies to go, but she waves her off. "I'm stuffed. Next time." She motions at me to walk out with her, but I can't leave like this.

"I'll catch up." I try to send her off without me, but she won't go until Olive shoos her out. They do that mysterious and horrifying thing where women communicate with just their eyes. I can see it happening, but I'm not sure what is passing between them. Della finally sighs and gives us a half-hearted wave as she leaves. She throws me one last threatening glare as the door closes behind her.

There are a few customers in the dining room and a handful of Olive's employees near enough to overhear us. "Could we talk outside for a minute?" I ask her. She crosses her arms over her chest, her sharp green eyes boring into me. For several seconds I'm convinced she's going to boot me out of her bakery, but she sighs and nods her head to the side door before stomping out ahead of me. I make an effort to suppress my grin as she huffs her way outside, her cute little ass bouncing with each step.

Olive rounds on me the second the door shuts. She comes at me with so much fire I almost take a step back. Almost. But I stand my ground even when she jambs a finger in my chest. "The only reason I let Della talk me into hiring you is because she says you're the best man for the job, and probably my only chance to get my classes running in time for the summer."

I cock an eyebrow, surprised that Della went to bat for me like that. She's right that I'm the best man for the job, but I know other guys could get it done in time too. And I know she knows that. I opt for a half-truth.

"She's not wrong. I am the best man for the job. Look, I wanted to apologize for what I said before. I didn't mean for it to come out the way it did. I just meant that I've been nothing but professional with clients before you…"

Olive sparks again, holding out a hand as she interrupts me. "Great!" Her voice is too high and way too chipper. "So you can do this job for me and be one hundred percent professional from now on, yes?"

I reach to take her hand without thinking about it but catch myself, dropping my arm back to my side. I want to slide my hands down her arms and calm her, but I doubt she would find it professional. I flex my hand, my fingers are itching to feel her skin again. "Is that really what you want from me?" I ask her.

She hesitates, and I don't miss the way her gaze darts to my lips. It's only a second, but I recognize the heat in her eyes before she puts her walls back up. She's blushing fiercely and maybe it's because I piss her off, but I don't think so. I'd bet big that she wants me as badly as I want her.

"Yes, that is exactly what I want from you." She holds up her fingers and counts on them: "One, keep your damn hands to yourself. Two, get my addition done on time. And three, be professional while you do it. Three things. That shouldn't be too hard, right?"

A lot of things shouldn't be as hard as they are, including my dick, which I'm having to hide behind my bag like a teenage boy. She's beautiful and so fucking tempting when she's fired up. I can only imagine how amazing all that pent-up passion would be when redirected…

Shit. I'm staring at her again. I try to clear the roughness from my throat, but my voice still comes out hoarse. "Yes, I can do all of those things, Olive." I can do all those things. And I will until I can convince her to change two of those three rules.

Chapter 9: Olive

Infuriating man. When I get back to work, Lilah and Luis won't stop watching me, likely waiting to see if I will snap. I know I have a temper, but it's not like I'm a bomb ready to go off when jostled. I'm tougher than that.

And, okay, maybe I was a tiny bit horrible to Brooks. I'm well aware that I don't handle rejection well. It's why I never date. Lashing out because he made me feel unwanted might not be the most adult reaction, but he hurt my feelings.

Ignoring my audience, I push Brooks out of my head and bury my feelings in my work. I sink myself into the flow of the bakery and do not think about him at all. I don't think about his dark blue eyes as I'm scaling out ingredients. I don't daydream about his lips on mine while I'm making pastry cream. I sure as hell don't look at my hands as I shape tart shells and wonder what his hands would feel like gripping my hips. I fill tiramisu jars and I most certainly don't fantasize about Brooks filling me.

After a few hours of this, I'm losing my mind. I have to get out of here. I'm going to scream if I have to spend one more minute trying to look zen while the last 24 hours play on repeat in my head. I just want to lose my shit in peace.

I check in with the front-of-house staff and head upstairs. I live in the apartment over the bakery and keep my office up here where I'm less likely to be distracted. There's never a shortage of behind-the-scenes work in a bakery like this and I like to do it alone.

I crank up some background music, send out an order to my grocery supplier, make the schedule for the next two weeks, reply to emails, and compile recipes for new desserts. I send everything to the printer, and then I can relax.

At least, I try to. I sit down with my Kindle, intending to read, but my mind keeps wandering. To a man who doesn't even fucking want me. To a man who regrets kissing me. I make a growling sound in my throat and toss my reader aside. Wine might not be an actual solution, but I pour myself an extra-large glass before sinking back down on the couch and staring at the ceiling feeling sorry for myself.

And that is how Lilah finds me.

Regaining consciousness, the first thing I feel is someone taking something out of my hand. Then my sister is whispering, "Pad Thai. Wake up for Pad Thai." The smell of peanuts and fish sauce and lime sink in faster than her words and I groan. I'm so hungry. My rumbling stomach is enough to bring me the rest of the way into the land of the conscious.

Laughing, I realize I fell asleep, wine in hand. Thank goodness Lilah took it before waking me up all the way. My vintage couch may be ugly as shit, but it's the most comfortable thing in the world. No need to spill perfectly good wine on it.

Lilah holds my wine glass back out to me with a wry smile. "Can you be trusted with this, Ollie?"

"Don't call me that. You know I hate that nickname." I take my glass back, trying to give her a haughty look but since I just woke up drooling on my couch with a crick in my neck, I'm sure it lacks the desired effect. Lilah rolls her eyes at me and pulls out cartons of takeout.

"Thank you for dinner. That was nice of you," I tell her as I reach out and squeeze her hand.

"Oh, I'm not being nice." She gives me a truly devious grin. "I'm waiting to hear the dirt."

"And all you brought was Pad Thai? It won't be enough to pry all the details out of me."

Lilah doesn't answer but gives me a precarious smile, her mouth stuffed with noodles as she reaches behind her and pulls a bottle of Chardonnay out of her bag.

She hands it to me and I nod. "Yeah, ok, that ought to do it."

It doesn't take long to fill her in. No one understands me better than Lilah. Our childhood was a hot mess. When I was six and Lilah was four, mom died in a car accident and then our sperm donor of a father abandoned us. Just dropped us off at our grandmother's house and never came back. Now Lilah has trust issues and I don't cope with rejection well. Needless to say, we don't date much. Therapy has worked wonders, and I know we both like to think we are both fully actualized adults, but works-in-progress is probably more accurate.

In some ways, I think we got off easy compared with our brothers. Asher, my twin, is our eldest sibling, even if only by 23 minutes. He grew up overnight, feeling responsible for everyone's happiness and safety. And younger brother, Lukas, went through a wild streak the likes of which Wine Country has yet to see again.

Our baby sister Julia was only two when our world imploded so she doesn't remember either of our parents and she's the only one who seemed to escape the emotional scars the rest of us are still working through.

Lilah and I work our way through the wine and spend the evening watching stupid movies. By the time I tuck myself into bed, I finally feel like I'm back on solid ground.

For the most part, I should be able to avoid dealing with Brooks in person. Email should cover any necessary communication, right? I probably won't even see him for at least a week or two. Which is good. Because I do not want to see him. At least this is what I tell myself as I drift off to sleep.

Three days later…

It's been one of those mornings. Front of house is understaffed after not one, but two people called out sick. The door of my convection oven broke so we have to rig it shut with a broom handle until the oven guy can come fix it. On top of all of that, I tripped and dropped a bowl of buttercream, denting an expensive Kitchen Aid bowl and splattering Swiss buttercream across the entire kitchen. If you haven't had to clean buttercream out of every nook and cranny in a commercial kitchen before, well, good for you. It sucks. It took me nearly an hour to make sure I got everything.

I'm behind schedule, which I fucking hate. Trying to quash my sour mood, I step out the side door to take a breath of fresh air. I sigh deeply and scroll through my phone to call in reinforcements for the servers. It takes four phone calls and a small bribe, but I get one of my servers to come in on his day off.

Overwhelmed and overtired, I sit on the step, put my head between my knees, and give in to the stress that's been strangling me all morning. It's not a tough girl thing to do, sitting outside and crying like this, but sometimes it's the only thing that makes me feel better. I don't know how else to let out the bottled up anxiety and pressure that comes with running a business on my own.

I cry myself out and I'm sure I look awful. I'm not a pretty crier like Lilah. When she cries, she gets these big teardrops that wet her eyelashes and fall neatly down her cheeks. My face goes all red and splotchy the second my tear ducts start up. I'll be puffy for hours but my crying fit was cathartic. I feel better. Wiping my face clean, I take a deep breath and let it out before hopping up and giving my whole body a shake, rolling my shoulders and letting all the bullshit go.

Chapter 10: Brooks

I woke up this morning and couldn't get her out of my head. I've spent the last three days wondering what Olive is doing and trying to decide the best way to approach her again. I laid there in bed trying to push thoughts of her out so I could just get a little more sleep. Instead, I was tormented by fantasies of Olive. Olive in her blue dress. Olive in her chef coat. Olive unbuttoning her chef coat. I had to get out of my house. I knew that if I didn't see her today, I was going to drive myself crazy.

Pulling into the bakery parking lot, I drive around to the side lot and back into a spot under a large oak tree. I'm just about to get out when Olive steps out of the side door talking on her cell phone. Her brows are drawn and the little scowl she's making is adorable. I'm torn between interrupting her and watching her. She makes a couple quick phone calls, her frown deepening with each call until it looks like she gets an answer she likes.

Grabbing my laptop I start to get out but I freeze when I see Olive sit on the step and pull her knees up, hugging them and hiding her face. Fuck. She's crying. I don't know what to do. I want to fix whatever is wrong, but I'll probably just make it worse. She doesn't trust me. At least not yet.

I worry a hand through my beard weighing my options, but just as I decide to get out and comfort her, she stands and wipes her face. She takes a deep breath and does a full body shimmy before straightening her chef coat and going back inside. I don't know what the fuck that was, but it was cute as shit.

I head around to the front door, climbing the steps two at a time. When I get to the front of the line, the baker, Luis, is putting bread in the display thing. He glares at me.

I try being friendly. "Hey, I didn't get to meet you the other day. I'm Brooks. My company is managing the addition."

"I know who you are. What do you want?" he asks irritably.

Well, this isn't going well. "I just wanted to see Olive for a minute. Check on her."

His eyebrows pinch together. "Check on her? She's busy. It's been a rough morning. I don't want you upsetting her again."

"Yeah… I saw her outside. Why was she crying?" I ask.

Luis squints one eye at me, thinking hard for a second. "Look man, that's just Olive. Sometimes she just needs to cry. She's tough as shit, but this place is a lot for one person to manage."

I open my mouth to respond, but he cuts me off. "The Donovan kids grew up next door to me and my boys. I've known Olive all her life and trust me when I tell you that she doesn't need you to fix her problems."

"I'm not trying to fix her problems. I just want to see her. That's all."

Luis eyes me suspiciously. "About the addition?"

I shake my head, not wanting to lie. "I just need to see her."

Luis raises an eyebrow. "Oh man, you've got it bad. Good luck with that. I'll tell her you're here but that's it." He laughs as he walks back towards the kitchen.

Chapter 11: Olive

I'm only back inside for a couple of minutes before Luis comes strolling into the kitchen. He's whistling loudly and grinning at me from ear to ear. Oh lord. This can't be good.

He props his elbows on my workbench, resting his chin on his fists and watches me spin the cake table as I carefully level the buttercream on the top of my cake. I have a dozen more to ice and I've wasted half of my morning already, so I try to ignore him. He stands his ground and clears his throat.

"Can you be helped, Luis?"

"Oh, Olive. I think it is you who might need help." He seems to be on the verge of giggles.

"Really? Because I'm pretty sure I could buttercream a cake in my sleep these days."

"Oh, Olive. It is not the cake that you need help with." He's not going to let this go, I guess. Sighing, I put down my offset spatula, cross my arms, and lean a hip on the counter.

"Fine, I'll bite. What has you grinning like the fucking Joker?"

Luis feigns a pained expression, holding a hand over his heart. "Oh, you wound me, my little friend!"

"Dude! Spit it out! I have so much work to do and I just want to get this done!"

Luis chuckles. He knows I'm not mad. "You have a visitor in the dining room. I told the girls up front not to put on Bon Jovi or they would get more of a show than they bargained for."

Oh, fuck me.

"Luis, are you trying to tell me Brooks is out front? And this is the way you want to share that information? You realize I'm your boss, right?"

He laughs and shakes his head as he heads back to his bread corner. "And you would never fire an old man like me."

"Start the sourdough for tomorrow please!" I slam down my decorating tools and stomp towards the front. And, because I'm a child, I call out a half-assed parting shot. "You're lucky I can't run this bakery without you!"

Luis dumps his bread dough out onto the floured surface, chuckling to himself. This is what happens when you hire someone who is basically family. He knows I would never fire him. Gran would kill me if I did, and I can't make bread the way he does.

Leaving him, I peek out front to see if he was just messing with me. I'm hoping, no, praying this is a joke. It's the kind of thing he might do. My hopes are dashed to pieces on the rock hard body sitting in my dining room.

Fuckity fuck. Nope.

It's only been three days, and Brooks is back in my cafe. I was so sure I wouldn't have to see him again for weeks. Surely, the embarrassment of stripping in front of me would have been enough to earn me a buffer? His visit can't be business related because I haven't even gotten plans back from Della yet. So why is he here?

And why the hell does he have to look so yummy? He's wearing dark jeans and a gray flannel shirt, and those jeans hug his thighs, accentuating how thickly muscled they are. The flannel fits across his broad shoulders and as he moves, I can see the muscles flex under it. Do they make flannel spandex blends now? Because if there's no stretch in that fabric, I'm worried his arms will just Hulk-rip their way out of the sleeves. Not that I would complain if they did.

His inky blue eyes flash as he types on the laptop in front of him, set off by his stupid dark gray shirt. Whatever he's working on seems to annoy him because his jaw ticks and the movement sparks a desire to run my hands through his short beard to see if it's as soft as it looks.

One of his hands leaves the laptop and his fingers slide up and down the handle of the mug absentmindedly. God, the things those fingers could do to my body…

One of my baristas steps out from behind the counter with a coffee carafe. Her eyes are locked on Brooks and she is oblivious to me and everyone else in the cafe as she refills his coffee cup. He barely looks up at her but she hovers over him asking if she can get him anything else. Oh, Jesus Christ. I'd like to shake her and tell her to have some self-respect, but I can't blame her.

She finally leaves him alone and returns to her post looking a little dejected. Something in me purrs at the way he ignored her flirty advances. Hmph. Stupid, really. Even if he were interested in Allison, it shouldn't matter. Except it does matter to me and I absolutely hate that I care. I wiggle my jaw to release the tension that's crept into my neck and is making me grind my teeth.

My phone dings in my pocket with a text message, making me jump. A startling reminder that I'm still hiding in the hallway. Fumbling to unlock my phone, I expect to see a message from one of my sisters but the name on my screen sends fire racing through my bloodstream.

Davidson Construction: "Stop spying on me and come have a coffee instead."

Me: "I'm not spying. I'm supervising. How did you get my number?"

I peek around the corner again, and Brooks is still looking down at his laptop, typing away. His phone is nowhere to be seen and just when I am sure this is a joke one of my employees is playing on me, he looks straight up at me, a hint of a smile in the corners of his blue eyes. He raises one finger and then plunks a key on his keyboard.

My phone buzzes in my hand, breaking the spell his eyes have put me under. I duck back into the hallway.

Davidson Construction: "Looks like spying from here... I got your number from the forms you filled out. I keep all my clients' numbers saved on my phone so I can confront them about skulking in the shadows. If you join me for coffee, I can show you some ideas I have for your classroom."

I can hear my heartbeat pounding in my ears and little tingles run over my skin.

Me: "It only looks like skulking because you know nothing about running a bakery. I have to make sure everything runs smoothly up front."

Poking my head back out, I see him shake his head. He's grinning. It's the first time I've really seen him smile. He's usually all stern and intense. But god, his smile. He's so fucking handsome when he grins like that. It makes my heart do strange and dangerously floppy things in my chest. I can hear my heartbeat pounding in my ears and little tingles run over my skin. I can't help grinning back.

I might admit, if only to myself, that I'd love nothing more than to go out there and sit with him. My whole body longs to be close to him. It's a terrible idea, of course. I'm the one who drew the line in the sand. This is a professional working relationship. It's what I asked him for, and he made it clear it's what he wants too.

So there's no way I'm going out there. That's just setting myself up for failure and heartbreak.

Me: "I have to get back to work. Enjoy your breakfast."

I head straight back to the kitchen without looking to see how he reacts. My phone vibrates in my pocket against my leg, but I ignore it and go back to my cakes.

Chapter 12: Brooks

The drive to Sonoma was worth it, if only to watch her peek around the corner at me with jealousy flashing in her eyes. Like the little barista was any kind of competition.

Rubbing my beard absentmindedly, I wonder if Olive will feel the need to oversee the dining room again anytime soon. All signs point to no. At least I got a smile out of her. That's progress, right? Sighing, I slide my laptop back into my bag and finish my coffee. I have to get back to Napa to meet up with Dan, one of my site managers. I watch for any sign of Olive as I walk to my car, but she stays in the kitchen, out of sight.

Things are fine in Napa, but for the first time I can remember, my heart isn't in my work. I'm distracted and I can tell I'm annoying the hell out of Dan. By the end of the day, he looks like he wants to strangle me.

"What the fuck is up with you today, man?" he asks, slapping a hand on my shoulder as we head out.

"I'm fine," I mutter.

"Bullshit, my dude. Your head wasn't here for five minutes today. You almost shot yourself in the foot with a nail gun, you started painting the wall the wrong damn color, and I caught you staring into space twice. I don't know what's up with you, but you better get your head straight before you come back on one of my sites."

I can't help smiling inward at his warning. He's a good guy, and he's right. I nearly nailed my foot to the floorboards today, but that doesn't mean I can let him give me a hard time. He wasn't any better when he met his wife a couple years back. She had his head spinning so hard that he tiled an entire bathroom with the wrong damn tile. He was lucky as hell the client liked it better than her original pick.

"You realize I'm your boss, right? Like, you understand who cuts your checks and assigns your crew the jobs?" Dan just grins at me. I shake my head at him. "I'll be fine. I just need to sort some shit out."

The real problem is that I don't know how to get Olive off my mind, especially heading into a job where I'll be near her almost every day. Close enough to smell the vanilla scent that drifts off her skin…

I catch myself spacing out again. Dan is already halfway to his car laughing at me and shaking his head. "Sort that shit out quick, man," he calls over his shoulder.

Growling to myself, I run my hands through my hair. I'm so damn irritated. At Dan. At Olive. Mostly at myself. I know I was callous and I hurt her feelings. Worst of all, I'm not sure how to fix it because she won't even talk to me.

I don't know what to do.

I've never felt this way about a woman before. I've dated a few, but it was nothing serious. We never really clicked. So even though it was easy with those women, it was unsatisfying.

Maybe it's part of the reason I like Olive so much. Nothing about her is easy. But if I could earn her affection, I know she'd be worth it. The pull I feel towards her doesn't go one way. I could see it in her eyes too. I just need to get her to forgive me, to show her I'm not the guy she thinks I am.

She's just so damn skittish. The only solution I can see is patience. Scrubbing my hand over my beard I groan. I'm usually a patient man, methodical to a fault, but Olive makes me feel out of control. Patient is the last damn thing I want to be.

Chapter 13: Olive

Davidson Construction: "You baking those lemon poppyseed muffins this morning?"

It's 6:30 in the morning and Brooks is texting me again. He knows I bake those muffins every morning. He knows this because he's been here nearly every day for the last two weeks. Usually, it's for breakfast. He sits and works at the same table, drinking coffee with half and half, no sugar, and eats a lemon poppyseed muffin. If he's in a hurry he pops in, grabbing lunch or coffee and a pastry to go.

But it doesn't matter what time he's here or how long he stays because he texts me every single time and asks me to have coffee with him.

And I'm a wuss because I always have an excuse. I'm too busy with the bakery, I'm about to leave, or I have a meeting. I've almost said yes so many times but I can't unsee the way he looked at me in horror when he realized who I was. I can't un-hear him calling our kiss a mistake. It shoots ice through my veins, reminding me why I can't spend time with him. So I say no. Over and over and over again.

I used to rotate muffin flavors. Lemon poppyseed used to be a Monday special; but ever since Brooks started coming in and asking for them daily, I added them to our daily bake schedule. I've told myself that it's just good business because they sell like crazy, but deep down I just want Brooks to eat those muffins and think of me.

I wonder if he's having to work out to burn off all those extra muffins. I can just see him hauling lumber around, sweaty and shirtless… Stupid distracting man! Shaking my head and clucking at myself for being so easily sidetracked, I text him back.

Me: Yup.

Davidson Construction: Save me a couple. I'll see you soon.

Oh god. Soon. Heat pours through my body at the thought. Today is the day his crew starts work on my addition, meaning Brooks will be in the building for hours on end, every day for the next several months.

I know I can't keep avoiding him. Over the last few weeks, I've pushed all of our interactions to email and text, which is perfect because I can't lose myself in his eyes or breathe in his delicious woodsy scent. But those days are over and I'll have to figure out how to not drool over the big jackass.

I'm exhausted just thinking about it. I'm already struggling to keep him out of my head. Now I have to spend the next few months working twice as hard to be professional and keep my stupid crush on Brooks to myself.

I spend the next hour finishing desserts for the pastry case. Danishes get glaze, apple turnovers get baked, and I'm just putting the chocolate curls on the mousse when Lilah enters the kitchen. She hangs up her coat and puts on her apron and hurries to the sink to wash her hands.

"Good morning," I smile at her.

She's early and there are dark circles under her eyes. I know she was bartending until at least midnight last night but she replies with a cheerful "Morning!" She washes her hands and heads straight to the freezer, pulling out trays of muffins to bake.

"Where's the fire?" I ask.

"Hot contractor man and his crew are up front demolishing the muffin supply. I figured I should bake another round or we won't have any left for the regulars."

"Jesus, seriously? How many of them are there? I baked two dozen extra already." I expected to sell a little extra with the construction workers hanging around, but I guess I underestimated the muffin demand.

Lilah gives me a pleased smile. "At this rate, you'll make enough money off the crew to pay for the addition." Her smile turns a little devious, and she cocks an eyebrow at me adding, "Brooks said he needs to talk to you before they start working."

"Of course he does," I mutter. I swear that man is determined to stir me up. I force a smile for Lilah. "I'll be back soon," I tell her. "Thanks for baking the muffins. Luis is on break. When he comes back can you please tell him we need an extra batch of sandwich rolls for lunch?"

She nods and gets to work, but I know she's watching me out of the corner of her eye as I hang up my apron and try to settle my nerves. For the millionth time, I curse Brooks for being so attractive. It would be a lot easier to deal with him if I didn't feel so damn drawn to him.

"Have fun!" Lilah croons in a sing-song tease. I don't even look back as I flip her off, making her giggle.

Chin up, shoulders straight, I walk into the dining room like I own the place, which I mother-effing do. Brooks stands at the register in his usual uniform of dark jeans and a dark flannel button down. The soft black material practically begs to be touched. I can't help but notice the way it sets off his blue eyes and dark beard. Pursing my lips and sighing, I'm already disappointed with myself. What happened to professionalism, Olive?

He looks up at me, and his serious expression melts into an enormous grin. God, his smile is everything. It sends my insides fluttering and my pulse racing. It crosses my mind that I don't think I've ever seen him smile like that for anyone else… but of course, that's stupid. I barely know him. I'm sure he smiles at other people all the time. I just don't see it because I'm too busy hiding from him.

"Morning Olive," he rumbles in a quiet baritone, holding out a hand for me to shake. His eyes crinkle at the corners, the only tell for the amusement he's hiding. Hesitating, I eye his huge hand. I know it's a trap. He shakes my hand every chance he gets so I know exactly what will happen. His hand will envelop mine and the warmth will spread up my arm until I shake him loose. My stupid betrayer of a heart will race long after I manage to get my hand free.

He knows what he's doing, I can see the challenge in his eyes. It's a game and I'm not sure I want to play. I can't win here. If I don't shake his hand, then I'm the one being unprofessional. I'm admitting he has that influence over me. Or at least, over my body.

I'm not weak and I won't give in, so I steel myself and take his hand, intending to shake it hard and pull free quickly. Brooks seems to have other ideas because he clasps my hand, holding it in both of his. It's intimate. Annoyingly so. But I still let that delicious warmth wrap around my hand, soaking it up before trying to take my hand back.

Even as I tug discreetly, I know he will hold on, refusing to let me go. Fine. If he's going to be a dick about it, he'll see how much patience I have for this kind of bull shit. I grip his hand as hard as I can, digging my nails in just a bit.

His eyebrows shoot up in surprise and I return his look with one of false innocence, batting my lashes at him. "Good morning, Mr. Davidson," I say sweetly.

He still doesn't let me go, instead he strokes my wrist with one of his fingers. I think it's meant to be a soothing gesture, but the reaction it causes in my body is anything but. My breathing stutters and I swear I can feel a finger stroke up my spine.

I wrench my hand free, making a show of it and letting his employees see him make an ass of himself. He doesn't seem to mind, but his eyes narrow thoughtfully. It clears an instant later, and he flags another man over to join us.

"Olive, this is Dan. Dan is the site manager for your build. I'll be here most of the time. I have meetings and other sites I'll have to check in on, but I'll be here as much as possible. Dan is my best guy." Brooks claps a hand on Dan's back. "Dan, this is Olive."

Dan is a friendly, thoroughly average looking man. He shakes my hand with a smile, and I look at Brooks as if to point out the professional way to shake a client's hand. Dan has a twinkle in his eye and looks pleased as punch when he says, "I've heard all about you, Olive. It's so nice to meet you!"

I eye Brooks, my jaw clenched so hard I think it might cramp. Surely, his crew doesn't know how we met. That would probably be more embarrassing for him than me.

Dan grins. "Brooks told us your bakery has the best coffee he's ever had."

Sighing with relief, I return Dan's warm smile. "That was… generous of him, but it is great coffee. I'm happy to meet you. Please let me know if you need anything from me. We're pretty slow right now so I don't think customers should get in your way."

"Thanks Olive. I'm going to snag some of those cupcakes to take home for the wife. She's pregnant and craving chocolate." He's glowing as he talks about his wife. It's sweet, and it makes my heart pang a little. It's not jealousy. Not really. I'm just trying to imagine what it must feel like to be so cherished and adored. No one has ever glowed like that when they talked about me.

I give his arm a brief pat. "I'll box up a dozen for you, on the house."

He starts to argue, but I interrupt him. "Please, it will make me happy to send them to her. I bake because cookies and cupcakes make people happy. And no one appreciates a chocolate cupcake like a pregnant lady."

Dan laughs, "I'll just have to do an extra good job for you then. Thank you, Olive. I really appreciate it." He gives us a little wave and leaves us to round up his crew. The tables are full of big burly men daintily eating muffins and scones and sipping coffee from pretty mugs. The sight makes me incredibly happy.

And then my attention is pulled back to Brooks as I feel a finger stroke my wrist. I whip my head back towards him only to realize he's stepped closer. I have to lean my head back to look up at him. His subtle scent fills the surrounding air, and because I'm weak, I lean in and breathe him in. God, he smells so damn good.

"I knew you liked me," Brooks smirks. I yank my hand away from him for the second time today.

"I most definitely do not like you," I snap back. "Keep your gigantic hands to yourself."

He chuckles and holds his hands up in a show of acquiescence. "Look, we're going to get started out back. We'll do our best not to disrupt business and I'll let you know ahead of time when we need to bring in any big equipment. I'll make sure they do deliveries before you open and you still have enough parking, ok?"

We've already discussed all of this through email, but I appreciate it. The last thing I want to do is chase off my regulars while we build out the extra space. So I nod and give him a tight smile. He reaches out to touch my face but stops an inch away, giving me a rueful smile and gesturing at his own forehead instead.

"You have flour, right here." Then he turns, tucking his hands into his pockets and heads outside with his crew. Cocky man. I most definitely do not like him and I certainly do not stare at his amazing ass as he walks out.

Chapter 14: Brooks

My guys are hard at work getting the area ready for the foundation. I trust Dan to make sure things run smoothly but I jump in and help, giving direction when needed and double checking everything that is being done.

I like knowing that Olive is right inside. I keep catching glimpses of her through the windows and she's hard at work, focused on whatever is in the mixing bowl. My thoughts drift back to the way she gripped my hand. I know she was trying to get a rise out of me and it worked.

Shaking her hand is the only time I get to touch her and even though she always puts up a show of pulling away when I hold on just a little too long, I can tell she likes the way we feel together. She fights it, but her eyes soften and she leans into me for just a second before remembering that she's not supposed to like it. I'm pretty sure I even caught her sniffing me this morning.

I'm not a dick, even though she might think I am. If I wasn't positive she liked me, I would let it go. At least I think I would. She's hiding behind her denial and pithy comments, but I'm going to draw her out.

We work hard until lunchtime, cranking through most of what we need to finish today to stay on track. We break for an hour and everybody splits in different directions, a few of the guys heading inside.

I spot Olive laughing with the girl running the cash register. Checking my watch, I set my laptop down at my favorite table before joining the line and ordering my lunch. As I pay, Olive eyes me. She looks like she's trying to make her mind up about something. Or maybe it's suspicion. With her, it's hard to tell sometimes. I see her face shift as she decides and waves me over to the other end of the counter.

She crosses her arms and leans a hip on the edge of the bar, her lips pursed as I walk towards her. She's so closed off, but my heart still thumps in my chest. In three weeks, this is the first time she initiated any of our conversations. Please God, don't let her be pissed at me for something new.

She chews on her bottom lip as I give her a grin. "Hey." I sound cool and collected as I go to lean a hand on the counter. And completely fucking miss it. I almost face plant on the ground but save myself just before going down.

Olive's eyes widen and her hands shoot out to catch me, her tiny hands wrapped around one of my biceps.

"Jesus, are you ok?" She giggles. She actually giggled. And it was the cutest thing I've ever heard in my life. She's still holding my bicep so I flex it under her grip, clearing my throat and laughing a little.

"Yup, I'm fine. No one's ever called me graceful." I hate how cold my arm feels when she lets me go but at least she's still smiling. I smooth my shirt and exaggerate, making a point of looking at the counter as I lean on it.

"What can I do for you, Olive?"

She grins at me for a second before looking around the dining room. "I wanted to do something nice for the guys working on my addition. Could you tell them coffee and muffins are on the house tomorrow morning?"

Jesus, she's so sweet. "That's really generous, are you sure? They can put down a lot of coffee."

She nods. "Yeah, I'm sure. I'm like the dealer of sweet breakfast pastries. Gotta give the buyer a little taste and get them hooked."

"A little taste, huh?" I cock an eyebrow at her, and she blushes. Ooh, what dirty thoughts are running through her mind? I'd kill to find out, but I'm doing my best to be respectful, if not entirely professional.

Just then we're interrupted by one of her employees setting down two plates on the counter. I can't remember her name. Alice, maybe? Whatever-her-name-is points to my French dip and fries and leans over the counter, batting her lashes at me. "Here's your lunch, Mr. Davidson."

I have to fight the urge to roll my eyes at her. What is she, like 18? Hard no. I gesture to the other plate with the panini and bowl of soup. "Who's this for?" It must come out colder than I meant to sound because Ashley-Alice-Aubrey pulls her shit together and stands up straight.

"Oh, Olive! This is yours."

Olive gives her an annoyed look but thanks her and sends her back to work. Before she can stop me, I pick up both plates and take them to my table.

"Excuse me, are you stealing my lunch now?" Olive asks as she follows me.

"No, you're finally going to sit with me. No excuses. You were going to eat alone, anyway. I'm not so horrible that you can't stand to sit with me for an hour, am I?"

She scoffs. "An hour? No way. I have to get back to work. I usually just eat standing in the corner of the kitchen."

I set her food down and pat the chair next to mine. "Thirty minutes. I can negotiate."

She chews on her lower lip and I expect her to argue, but she surprises me and sits. She huffs and mutters, "Fine," under her breath, but I'll take it.

"How did you get into baking?" I ask her before taking a bite of my sandwich and moaning. Jesus, she makes the best fucking French dip.

She finishes chewing an enormous bite of her panini before answering. "I started baking because it made my brothers and sisters happy. There wasn't a lot to be happy about when we were young, but cookies made everyone feel better. My Gran taught me a lot and then I went to culinary school and got my very overpriced degree in baking and pastry."

I frown at her. "Why weren't you guys happy as kids?"

"It's kind of a lot to unpack over sandwiches but basically, our mom died and our dad was a dick and then he left. It was a lot for us to deal with. We had Gran, but it wasn't the same after Mom died." She chews with a thoughtful expression on her face. I so badly want to reach out and hold her hand. She wouldn't like it. Not yet. I shift in my seat and let my knee touch hers. She doesn't pull away so at least I can get away with this. My chest feels tight, aching for the little girl she was and everything she lost.

"That sucks. I'm sorry."

She shrugs. "What was your childhood like?"

I laugh, but it's not a humorous sound. She's been honest with me, so I guess I can return the favor. "Cold? I don't know. It wasn't horrible or tragic, but my parents weren't the warm and fuzzy types. They were both lawyers. Very driven. They expected a lot out of me and let's just say construction doesn't cut it. Even if I own my own company."

Olive's mouth pulls to the side in a sympathetic expression. And maybe it's my imagination, but it seems like her knee presses back into mine just a little.

"Tell me about culinary school."

She brightens. "It was amazing. I got to do what I love all day, every day. I was surrounded by people who were as passionate about it as I am. It's part of the reason I love my bakery so much. That, and the fact that I'm in charge. Plus there are always fresh-baked cookies around, so it's almost perfect."

Chapter 15: Olive

Almost perfect?" Brooks asks.

"Well, yeah. I mean, it's stressful, too. All of my employees depend on me making good decisions. If I fuck up it's on me, but it affects them too."

Brooks nods. "I get that," he says. I hadn't thought about it, but I guess he would know exactly what that's like. "What are your favorite things to make?" he asks.

I could talk about baking all day, but most people will eventually zone out. Brooks doesn't seem to mind, though. He asks how we make the chocolates, how we roast the coffee, and even what my clients are like. He watches me like I'm the most fascinating thing he's ever seen and there's a soft smile playing around his lips. He looks content. It's flattering to have someone look at me like that. Flattering and a little unsettling. I roll my shoulders and change the subject, trying to get Brooks talking instead.

"Why did you get into construction?" I ask.

He chuckles. "To impress girls."

"Oh, come on!" I exclaim as I backhand his arm. "I gave you a real answer."

His smile crinkles the corners of his eyes in the most adorable way. "I'm serious. I wasn't any good at sports, but I'm great at math and science. I was a scrawny little nerd, and I wanted to do something manly over the summer between my junior and senior years of high school."

I take a bite of my panini and listen to the sound of his voice. It rolls over me easily; I think I could listen to him talk all day.

"We had a neighbor named Fred, who owned a construction company and let me intern with him. I loved it. I loved everything about it. So after high school I got my degree in Civil Engineering and worked with Fred for a couple of years. When he wanted to retire, I bought his company, renamed it, and made it my own." He's practically glowing with pride.

"Two things. One, that's adorable. I need to see pictures of scrawny adolescent you. Two, that sounds like a crazy amount of work."

Brooks scrubs his hand through his beard. "One, no way are you seeing those pictures. And two, yeah, it was a lot of work. All I've done for the past decade and a half is work. But I've seen the way you work around here and I can honestly say there's no way I could keep up with you."

I blush at the compliment. I'm having fun with him. Not that I'll admit it.

We sit in companionable silence and eat our lunch until Brooks nudges my elbow with his. "What are you smiling about over there?" he asks.

"I'm wondering if I can cyber-stalk you well enough to find your mom on Facebook and get her to send me those pictures." I tease back.

"Impossible. My mom doesn't have Facebook."

"Well, damn. Now I'm going to have to figure out another way." I pick up our empty plates and stand. "I have to get back to work. This was fun. Thanks. I didn't expect a stripper to have an engineering degree. I think you might be overqualified for dancing." His laugh comes out a booming bark behind me. I look back after dropping the plates off at the bussing station and he shakes his head at me, grinning.

I spend a few more hours doing prep work. Brooks is right outside the window and I have to try very hard to ignore him and focus on my baking. I can see him watching me. I steal glances when I know he's looking the other way. He's so tall and broad shouldered. I try, but I can't picture him as a skinny teenager. I bet he was adorable, though.

I head up to my apartment to take a nap. Lilah is passed out on my couch with the TV on, getting some much-needed rest. Thank god she came in early to help me or the breakfast pastries would have been decimated by 9 am. I would have been behind all day. I fluff a throw blanket over her before going to get a glass of water. The kitchen window overlooks the building area and I watch Brooks for way longer than I'd like to admit. I'm such a creeper.

***

One week later…

I'm losing my mind. Every day when I go to pick up my lunch, Brooks has already swooped in and set it at his table. And I let him. It doesn't even matter what time I put my lunch order in with the line because he's always there to snatch it up.

I know he's got a spy on the inside. There's no other way he would always know when my lunch is coming up. Someone is helping him. Probably more than one person, actually. I think my staff might be ganging up on me. As much as I hate to admit it, he's really grown on me and the idea that he's wrangling help to get to spend time with me is as flattering as it is crazy.

I've started to look forward to our lunches together. This is the most time I've ever spent with one man. I tried dating when I was in school, but there were no second dates. I had a couple casual hook-ups, mostly because I was curious. After a couple of very uninspiring experiences, I decided that dating and sex just weren't for me. I know I'm a little broken… but being with Brooks makes me feel a little less broken. And while I know the lunches aren't dates, and most of our conversations center on the build out, what his crew is working on next, and the specials I'm baking the next day, I get a silent thrill every time his knee brushes mine or our arms graze as we look at flooring samples together.

He keeps a straight face anytime we touch, his eyes impassive, but it seems like he bumps me more and more every time we sit together. I know my imagination is acting up and I have to remind myself daily to chill. It's clear the slight touches don't even register with Brooks. I'm just ridiculous.

This is a professional relationship. At least that's my inner chant. Professional. Professional. Professional.

But with each minute spent near Brooks, I feel less and less professional. I get more of his smiles, something no one else seems to get, and it gets harder to ignore my body's reaction to his nearness. It's starting to feel like torture to sit still next to him, aware of every move he makes and wondering if he feels even one tenth of what I'm going through. If he does, then he should have gone into acting because the man is cool as an ice cube.

***

Weekly dinner at my Grandma's house is as loud as ever. Being one of five kids has conditioned me to function well with chaos and noise. Most of my days are quiet at the bakery and I live alone, unless one of my sisters crashes on my couch. So even though I always look forward to our big family dinners, I'm happy to retreat to my apartment at the end of the night.

Gran pesters me about my dating life (non-existent) and the construction at the bakery. (Nothing to report yet.) Lilah gives me pointed looks with her eyebrows raised so high she looks like she fell victim to a bad facelift.

No way am I telling my Gran about my lunches with Brooks. She will blow it way out of proportion and start planning a wedding. I wouldn't put it past her to nose around the bakery trying to meet him.

"How do you like your contractor?" my brother Asher, asks. "We need some work done at the garage."

Sipping my wine and avoiding all eye contact, I reply, "Yeah, he's great. Very professional." Lilah snorts over her glass and starts to say something, but I interrupt her. "How's your last semester going? Are you ready to be a legit nurse?" I ask my little sister Julia.

Julia is only half awake, watching us with her chin supported on her hand. "One more week and then I can take the NCLEX. I'm still at the hospital with Rita, the demon nurse, but after next week I'm done. Thank god." She moans and puts her head down on the table. Yikes. Poor kid. Nursing school seems a lot more strenuous than culinary school. Less fun, too.

Dinner is just wrapping up when I feel my phone vibrate in my pocket. I check it under the table so Gran doesn't get salty about phones at the dinner table.

Davidson Construction: "Hey, sorry to bug you. I think I left my notebook in the bakery. Any chance you could let me in to grab it? I need it to place some orders tonight."

Shit. Asher drove me over and I don't have my car. I hate to ask him to leave early, but I don't have much of a choice. "Asher, can I beg a ride back to the bakery?"

"Why are you leaving so early?" Gran asks before Asher has time to answer.

"I'm sorry. It's the contractor. He left some work stuff at the bakery and needs it tonight." I avoid meeting Lilah's eyes, but I can almost hear her raising her eyebrows. Gran pouts, but Asher agrees to drive me back. Julia bolts for the door while Asher and I hug our grandmother. Gran starts to protest, but Julia blows her a kiss.

"I love you all, but if I don't get some sleep I'm going to die," she says before jogging to her car.

Gran shakes her head at Julia's retreating form. "I can't wait until that girl is done with school. You all owe me an extra long dinner next week."

"Extra long, I promise. I'll even bring your favorite carrot cake," I say as I kiss her on the cheek and we head out.

I text Brooks my E.T.A. as Asher and I chat about his car shop on the way back to my building. He and Lukas, our younger brother, opened a repair shop last year, and it's doing well. He tells me all about the repairs he's working on this week and 95% of it flies over my head. It doesn't matter. It's just nice to spend time with my brother.

"Are you sure you're ok alone with this contractor guy?" Asher asks as we pull into the bakery parking lot. "I can stay."

"Stop worrying," I say. "He wouldn't hurt me, I promise." I give Asher a kiss on the cheek before hopping out and waving him on his way. He still waits for me to get safely inside the side door to my apartment before leaving.

I pop upstairs to drop off my purse. Pouring myself a second glass of wine, I settle in to read while I wait for Brooks.

Twenty minutes later he texts me to say he's out front. That was quick. I sigh and toss aside my poor book. I'll never finish it. My post-apocalyptic dragon shifters deserve better. I skip down the stairs, bringing my last sip of wine with me, and go to the front door to let Brooks in.

Now that I'm thinking about it, I guess I should have looked for his notebook while I waited. Too late now. He gives me a lopsided grin as I gesture for him to come in. Between his masculine scent, the devilishly handsome look on his face, and the sudden realization that I'm alone with him for the first time, I'm glad I didn't look for the notebook. I'll take a few extra minutes alone with him, even if it's just hunting down the lost book.

"Thank you so much. You're a lifesaver, Olive." He says as he steps inside. His broad chest comes within a couple inches of me and my stupid nipples are trying to detach from my body to get to him. Mentally chastising them has absolutely no effect. Mutiny.

"I can't believe I forgot my notebook. I guess I was distracted." He tosses me a wink like I'm the great distraction. My cheeks heat up and I roll my eyes, fighting back the butterflies that seem to have escaped in my belly.

He heads over to his table. Funny that it's his table now, but it is.

"I don't think it will be there. I bet it's in the lost and found box." I tell him as I head towards the cashier station, tossing back the last sip of wine and setting my empty wine glass down on the counter. Sure enough, there's a black hardcover notebook right on top. I pick it up and slap it against my other palm.

Brooks looks so relieved. He holds a hand out for his notebook. "Thank you so much. Seriously. I don't know what I would do if I lost it."

"Hold up mister, I'm going to need to make sure this belongs to you. Company policy," I tease as I hold it behind my back. Brooks steps toward me slowly and I'm drowning in the intensity on his face.

"How am I supposed to prove it's mine?" he asks me, taking another measured step towards me. He approaches me carefully and with purpose. The way you would approach an animal you don't want to run away. I don't feel like running now, though. My heart, or at least my traitorous body, wills him to come closer.

Brooks holds my eye contact and steps right into me, his hips pinning mine into the counter. His scent washes over me and the delicious weight of his body against mine makes my head spin. He's enormous, and I have to crane my head back as I look up at him.

Maybe it's the wine, but I'm feeling brave. For the first time in a long time, I think I could let someone in. It's a big, scary thought. A risk I've never been willing, or able, to take. I shove down the little voice that's kept my walls up and protected me for so long. I can be brave. I can do this.

He reaches around me with both arms, placing one hand on the counter and wrapping the other around my back to take the notebook from my hand.

He brings the book out in front of me but doesn't move away as he flips the cover open with one hand and shows me his name and phone number written there.

"Satisfied?" he asks, with a soft, crooked grin. His eyes bore into me, piercing any reserve I had left. The air is charged between us and my body is carrying the current, making my breathing rapid and shallow. I'm staring at his mouth, the full lower lip tempting to the point of distraction.

Kiss me, kiss me, kiss me. I chant in my mind. I'd kiss him, but he's so tall I can't reach his lips. If I just had a damn step stool…

"Not even a little," I answer and reach up to touch his beard with one hand. I have been dying to run my hands over it for weeks and it's even softer than I imagined.

Brooks' eyes are heavy lidded and his arm wraps around my waist, pulling me tighter against him. I can feel his warmth seeping through me everywhere our bodies touch. He lowers his face and brushes his nose against mine. Our lips are so close I can feel his breath tickle my skin.

"Olive?" He rumbles my name, and it sounds like he's asking my permission. I've been fighting this feeling down for weeks and really, I don't want to fight anymore. I want to give in. I want to drown in it. Drown in him.

I slide my arms around his neck and close the distance myself, letting my lips graze over his. His lips are gentle as he kisses me back and heat spikes through my body, curling in my core, tingling out through my arms and legs.

Somehow this is better than the hard, lustful way he kissed me in the hotel. He's sweeter, almost reverent with me. It feels like he needs me as much as I've been needing him. Brooks cradles my body into his much larger one. It would feel cozy if not for the hard length pressing into my lower belly.

He licks my bottom lip, nipping at it softly and coaxing me to let him in. Until now, the heat between us was a sweet gentle fire; but now his tongue meets mine, and my body erupts with raging need. His thick thigh wedges between my legs and I'm moving against him.

My quiet moan is matched by his low growl. His fingers tunnel into my hair as I grind against him. More. I want so much more, but the sound of breaking glass interrupts us. Pulled from the moment, I look over my shoulder to see my empty wine glass broken on the counter behind me. One of us must have tipped it over.

I look back at Brooks, ready to laugh it off. His gaze slides from the glass back to me and I can see it in his eyes; the exact second he shuts down. It's written all over his tragically handsome face before he even moves a muscle. Regret.

A chill washes over my body and my stomach drops. What in the actual fuck have I done? Things were just getting comfortable between us. We could finally have friendly conversations. I was doing so well at shoving down my attraction for him, but now I've gone and fucked this all up.

Chapter 16: Brooks

I have her in my arms after weeks and weeks of wanting her. She's right here, willing and wanting me as much as I want her. She finally let her damn guard down.

That would be great, if she wasn't drinking.

But I can't be the asshole that takes advantage of her because she had one too many glasses of wine. So no matter how much my body cries out at the loss, I pull back. I put some distance between us. She watches me through wary eyes as I release her and run my hands through my hair.

Ignoring the taste of her on my tongue, the sweet vanilla scent of her skin, and the way her body curled into mine so perfectly, I try to do the right thing.

"I'm sorry, I--" I start to explain but Olive's face crumples in pain and anger, her chest heaving with emotion.

"Oh, really?! You're sorry? Again?!" She wrenches away from me. Storming towards the back staircase up to her apartment.

"Olive!" I bellow after her. "Just let me explain. I just didn't want--"

"Can you please just fuck off!"

She's out of sight in seconds and I'm left here alone as she slams the door behind her. What in the fresh hell just happened?! If she would just fucking listen to me for once and let me explain myself, none of this would even be an issue.

I knock on the door and when she won't answer and when I try the handle she's locked it. Infuriating woman.

"Shit," I mutter. Slapping my hand on the doorframe isn't the best response, but it makes me feel better for a minute. I scoop up my notebook from where I dropped it on the floor and pull my phone out of my pocket. I try to call her but it goes straight to voicemail so I send her a text message and hope she'll read it when she turns her phone back on.

Me: "I get that you're upset. Come back down so we can talk."

I wait for a couple more minutes but it's never marked as delivered or read. I don't want to leave, but sitting in the bakery all night won't do any good. Sighing, I clean up the broken glass. I let myself out the front door, making sure everything is locked up tight before I go. I'll come back and check on her first thing in the morning.

I drive home in a daze, half wishing I had sat in front of her door and waited for her to come back down. She needs some time to cool down. I think it would have been a mistake. She can't avoid me forever, but my patience is wearing thin.

Chapter 17: Olive

I lock the door behind me and run up the stairs, turning my phone off as I go. I can't hear or read one more word from him. I don't know why he changed his mind and at this point I just don't care. I know these are my issues to deal with, but I'm crushed.

Jesus, I can't breathe. I gasp for air as I slide down the wall. Misery washes over me and all I can do is let the sobs rip out of my chest.

What was I thinking? I opened myself up to this even though I knew it was a terrible idea. Except I know exactly what I was thinking. I thought Brooks was pursuing me the last few weeks. Clearly, he was just trying to get back to a friendly professional place and I've been reading him all wrong. I was thinking with my sex starved lady parts instead of my actual brain.

I'm wallowing. I feel pathetic and I'm so disappointed. Mostly with myself. And I'm embarrassed. I can't believe I did that and now I'll have to face him every day and pretend like I didn't try to climb him like a tree.

I'm tempted to call Lilah, but I don't want a pep talk right now. Instead, I leave my phone powered off, curl up in bed and cry myself to sleep like a child. I'll give myself this one night to flounder in my sadness and disappointment. Tomorrow I will pick myself up, put on my big girl panties, and get the fuck over my stupid crush on Brooks.

Chapter 18: Brooks

Sleep doesn't come easy, and I wake up to my 6am alarm feeling more tired than when I laid down. I struggle through a shower, praying Olive will be reasonable. Hah! Not likely.

She's making me crazy, but I'm not giving up. I admire so much about her. She's so damn smart and hard working. She's funny, beautiful ,and generous. I'm drawn to her like she's my own personal black hole. I can't escape her and I don't want to.

I was raised with very little affection. I've always thought I didn't need it. I never felt the need to be touched. For the first time, I feel desperate to be close to someone. I've been living for each glancing touch of her knee at our lunches. I realize now that I've been a starving man looking for crumbs. I need more. More of her touches and kisses. More everything.

I'm going to fix this. I just need to figure out how.

I'm at the bakery at 6:50, waiting by the front doors for someone to unlock them. The sun isn't up but I'm here. Olive can't run forever. I start pacing at 6:56, my breath coming in warm puffs in the chilly air. Just before 7:00 Lilah opens the door, unlocking it and giving me an exasperated look.

"Why are you out here pacing like a lion and scowling? The staff was afraid to open the door."

"I need to talk to Olive." I try to peer around her, but I don't see her anywhere.

Lilah gives me a suspicious look. "It's her morning off and she hasn't been down yet. You look like shit, by the way. What happened?" she asks.

"Nothing really happened. I just need to talk to Olive. Is she in the back?"
Lilah holds up a hand, refusing to let me pass her.

"I'm sorry. When you say, 'nothing really happened' do you mean nothing actually happened or do you mean something really did happen and you're just going to blow me off?"

I blink at her for a second, my lips pressed together in a hard line. I'm annoyed she's not letting me in and she's pressing me for information I don't want to give. It occurs to me that Lilah and Olive are close. Maybe she could help me not fuck this up entirely.

I hesitate because even though I'm willing to bet she could help. I'm not sure it feels right to get her involved. She raises an eyebrow at me and purses her lips. She's shorter and curvier than Olive, but their eyes are almost identical. "How about you tell me what you did and, if I think you deserve it, I'll help you."

I'll take that deal, I decide, nodding at her. She motions for me to stay on the front porch while she finishes unlocking the doors and flipping the sign to "Open." Then she joins me on the porch, crosses her arms, and gives me an impatient look. "Go on then. Let's hear it."

I grip the back of my neck with one hand and rub it, trying to ease the tension that has built up. "We kissed last night. She kissed me, or I kissed her. I'm not really sure." Her eyes go wide but she says nothing so I keep talking. "I stopped it because she'd been drinking. I didn't want to take advantage of her. She flipped out and bolted. She hasn't read my text messages or returned my phone calls. I just want to make sure she's ok. I just want to talk to her."

Lilah furrows her brows, giving me a calculating look. "Did you tell her why you stopped the kiss?"

"No, she wouldn't let me get it out before she took off."

Lilah looks exasperated. "So, the first time you kissed her you told her it was a mistake, and you never expected to see her again. Then you pursue her in a super lukewarm way. And when you finally, and I do mean finally, kiss her again, you end up pushing her away. Maybe you can see why she'd feel rejected? She had one glass of wine at our family dinner and unless she came home and slammed three more just so she could deal with your grumpy ass, I doubt she was drunk. You just assumed she was because she was carrying a wine glass and let her walls down a smidge. If you'd bothered to ask her, Olive would tell you that she never drinks more than a glass or two of wine. She's a grown ass woman and can handle two glasses of wine without turning into a self-destructive mess."

I nod, chagrined. She pinches the bridge of her nose and pauses, thinking.

"I'm not going to get in the middle of this because you two need to figure out your own shit. However, I will give you a piece of advice because I love my sister more than anyone else in this world. I want her to be happy and I think she could be with you. If you get this right."

"I'm listening," I say, trying not to sound as eager as I feel.

"Olive is extra sensitive to feeling unwanted. She doesn't handle rejection well. If you're not in this for the long run or you aren't sure, then you need to back off and leave her alone because I think you have the capability to really damage her."

I shake my head firmly and stare her down. "I want her. I've been trying to be patient with her and not scare her off, but I'm done with that shit. I'm all in."

She finally smiles at me and nods. "Good. Make sure you don't fuck up again because if you make my sister cry, I'll cut your balls off and feed them to you." She smiles at me sweetly. "And then I'll unleash my brothers on you."

"Jesus Christ, you're scary," I tell her. She smiles at me and walks back inside.

I scrub my hand over my face. I've been handling Olive all wrong, trying to be patient and let her come to me. Well, no more. She's all mine. Every inch of her. She just doesn't realize it yet.

Chapter 19: Olive

I roll over in bed with the sun streaming in through my useless curtains. It's so damn bright. I have a headache and my face feels puffy from crying. I am such a sad sack. Patting my hair, I can tell it's tangled beyond what a brush can take care of. I need a shower. Desperately. I'm pretty sure I look and smell like I went ten rounds with an angry gorilla and lost.

My phone is lying on the bed next to me, still turned off. I eye it, but I still don't feel like turning it on. I'd leave it off all day, but I'm never out of touch with my employees, even on my day off. I'll have to do it eventually, just not yet.

I thump my pillow over my face and scream into it until I feel better. I am going to pick myself up today. I'll clean myself up and stop feeling sorry for myself. Last night I made a stupid mistake, and I've learned my lesson. I can move on and be a grown up about this.

Grown up or not, I peek through the curtains carefully. My apartment overlooks the construction area and I need to know if Brooks is out there. I'm relieved when I don't see him right away. Maybe he's working at another site today. God willing, he will just stay off my property for the next few months.

I rinse off in the shower and wash my hair. I slather conditioner all over my tangles and let it sit as I run a nice hot bath. Digging around the cabinet, I find a bath bomb my sister gave me for my birthday. Bath bombs don't go bad, do they? It still smells good, so I have to figure it's fine. I toss that in the bath and sit down to soak away my embarrassment from last night.

After getting some sleep, I'm even more confused than I was last night. I'm not crazy and I don't think I was imagining the way Brooks looked at me. I certainly wasn't imagining the texts he sent every single day asking me to have coffee and sit with him. I didn't imagine the lunches together that he orchestrated and insisted on over and over again.

I don't know why he pulled away. I guess he just got carried away and realized he made a mistake. Again. I rub my chest, trying to ease the ache. I hate the way I feel, unwanted and weak.

But seriously, fuck that. I am not weak. I've protected myself this long. I just need to buck up, remember who I am, and why I keep my walls up.

I sit in the bath so long the water starts to get chilly and I'm pruny beyond reason. I get out, dripping all over the bathroom floor as I wrap up in my towel. Maybe I'll go shopping. I haven't seen Sally or Chelsea much since the bachelorette party and a new outfit might make me feel better.

I eye my phone. It's still sitting on the bedside table, powered off. I know I have to suck it up and turn it back on. I can't be out of touch with the bakery, especially with the ongoing construction. Powering it up, I see a pile of text messages and a voicemail from Brooks. I ignore all of it and open the text from my sister.

Lilah: "Brooks was looking for you this morning. He seems really upset. Maybe you should talk to him."

Oh Jesus. Has he gotten her on his side now?

Me: "No thanks. I'm going to Sally's. Dinner with Chelsea tonight at Harvest."

I throw on jeans and a hoodie, my hair in a messy pile on top of my head. At least I'm clean, if not presentable. I sneak out the side door after peeking out to make sure Brooks isn't lying in wait. I'm not sure if I'm relieved or disappointed that I manage to escape without him noticing.

It's a quick walk to Sally's boutique. She's working on a window display, wearing a black velvet swing dress with amethyst leggings and pointy black boots. It's not a look I could pull off, but I love it on her.

As I walk into the store, she looks me up and down and cocks an eyebrow.

"Because I love you, I'm going to tell you the truth. You look like hot garbage."

I laugh and let her pull me in for a hug.

"I know. It was a rough night. I need retail therapy." My voice is muffled into her shoulder as she squeezes me tight. She smells like jasmine, familiar and safe. I pull back and gesture at her outfit. "Love the velvet."

She twirls, letting the dress whoosh out. "It's witch chic," she says with a chuckle. "Want to talk about your shitty night?"

"Not really. I'm just in my own head. Where's Chelsea?"

"Oh, I gave her the day off. The wedding planner wanted to go over things with her again and it's been quiet here."

"Oh my god, again? That wedding planner is so neurotic. Oh well, I'm glad to see you. Want to play dress up, Elphaba?"

Sally cackles like a witch and pulls me farther into the shop. An hour later, I'm decked out in a short black leather skirt and a cream blouse layered with a forest green wrap cardigan and black suede ankle booties.

She eyes me as I pay her, putting a dent on my credit card. Thank god she gives me a discount.

"You still need to do something with your hair." She's blunt but I love her for it. I don't want to go home and risk running into Brooks but she's right, my hair is a mess.

Sally rubs her hands together before digging in her purse. "I know you said you don't want to talk about it but whatever is going on, but you know you can come to me anytime." She pulls out an envelope and hands it to me. "You need to relax and I will never get around to using that." Opening the envelope, I pull out a gift certificate for Francesca's Salon and Day Spa.

Tears well up in my eyes. "Sally… this is too much."

"Nonsense! You deserve it. You work your hands to the bone most days. There's enough there for a full package so go get a massage and get your nails and hair done. Treat yo self!"

I giggle, but she grabs my hand. "Olive, look at me." I meet her eyes as they bore into mine, "You deserve to be happy."

My eyes fill with tears and I give her a wobbly smile. God, she really knows how to get to me.

Chapter 20: Brooks

I hang around the bakery all morning, overseeing the foundation work and hoping Olive will at least come downstairs. I had planned to stay all day but just before lunchtime I get a phone call from one of my site managers.

"Hey man, what's up?" I ask him.

"Shit man, you've gotta get down here," he sounds exasperated and I can hear a woman screeching in the background.

I'm already collecting my stuff and heading for my truck as I ask him what happened.

"Mrs. Beaty let her three poodles outside and they tumbled into the foundation pad before the concrete set. She's flipping out about dogs needing to be professionally groomed even though one of my guys volunteered to clean them up. Honestly, the dogs are fine. I'm more worried about the pad. I'm not sure if we will have to redo the whole damn thing."

I race down to Napa. When I get there, a younger guy is cleaning the poodles, meticulously scrubbing the concrete out of their fur. The trio seem to be enjoying the extra attention. One of them is giving him a hard time, but he's doing ok.

After a quick assessment, the foundation pad is still soft. I put the crew to work fixing the poodle damage. Once the foundation is repaired, I help the kid dry the poodles with a towel and a mini air blower one of the guys had in his truck. The only thing left to deal with is Mrs. Beaty declaring I should pay for professional grooming.

This isn't my first rodeo with a client like this. I'll go pretty far out of my way to make a client happy, but I've got to draw the line somewhere. I tell her I'll be happy to pay for the grooming but if I do, she'll have to cover the repair cost to the slab and the extra time the crew was set back. Wouldn't you know it? It turns out the slab repair cost more.

We agree to call it even and move on with our day.

It's almost 5pm before I can head back up to Sonoma and check on Olive. Last night has been playing on repeat in my head. I still can't believe how far off the rails it went. I don't have a plan, but I'm not going another night without fixing this and making Olive see how much I need her.

Shaking my head to myself, I pull into the parking lot. My crew is packing up for the day, and the site looks great. Everything is on track so I clap Dan on the back and thank him before heading inside.

Olive is nowhere to be found, but in the kitchen I find Lilah putting on a coat and getting ready to leave. She spots me and gives me a calculating look before turning to Luis and declaring, "Olive is going to that little gastropub, Harvest, for dinner."

Luis gives her a confused look. "Okay… Why are you yelling at me about it?"

She smiles to herself. "Was I being too loud? Sorry, Luis. See you tomorrow."

She winks at me and gives me a conspiratorial smile as she walks outside.

Luis eyes me with distrust and looks around the kitchen. Seeing he and I are alone, he picks up his knife and shakes it at me.

"You know Olive and Lilah are like daughters to me, yes?" he asks.

I nod.

"Good," he continues. "Then you should understand that if you hurt either of them, I'll make sure you suffer."

Jesus, I've never been threatened so many times in one day. "Understood, sir." I give him a salute and back out of the kitchen. Heading into the chilly winter air, I pull out my phone and look up the address for Harvest.

Chapter 21: Olive

I spent the afternoon getting pampered, polished, and cleaned up. My muscles are relaxed, my toes have a fresh coat of red polish, and my outlook on life is significantly improved. Even my hair looks happier.

I feel a million times better than when I fell into bed last night. I strut into the restaurant swinging my leather clad hips and feeling like a badass. Chelsea isn't here yet, so I give the hostess my name and wait at the bar. I flag the bartender and order a glass of Prosecco before checking my phone. I missed a text from Chelsea.

Chelsea: "Some jackass rear-ended me. I have to get my car towed. Not going to make it."

Well, shit.

Me: "That sucks! Are you ok? Do you want me to come pick you up?"

Chelsea: "I'm fine. Matt is already on his way. Rain check on dinner?"

I let out a disappointed sigh but send her the thumbs up emoji. Knowing Matt, he won't let her out of his sight for the rest of the night.

On my own. Again. After the disappointment of last night I'm still a little raw and despite my amazing day I'm still feeling a little down. Lonely. Well, lonely and hungry. My stomach rumbles loudly. All I've eaten today was a smoothie at the spa and that is NOT enough. I order some blistered Shishito peppers and a charcuterie plate and open the Kindle app on my phone. I might as well enjoy my alone time.

I'm so wrapped up in my book and my food that I don't even notice the man sitting next to me until he interrupts a very steamy scene.

"What are you reading?" he asks, jarring me back from an icy planet far, far away. He's good looking in a generic way. I tip my phone away from him, making sure he can't see what I was reading. Somehow I don't think he'd appreciate the sexy sci-fi romance as much as I do.

On a scale of one to ten, I wonder how rude it would be to just ignore him and go back to my story. But I'm not a total dick and, even though I don't want to, I answer him. Sort of.

"A book." I say flatly before going back to my phone.

"Is it a good one?"

I sigh and pointedly put my phone down on the bar before looking back up at him. He's got a Ken Doll thing going on. I'm sure it works for him most of the time.

"It is a really good book but I'm pretty sure it's not your thing. I'm also guessing you're not going to let me focus on it."

He chuckles and gives me a grin that would probably charm the panties off most straight women. Me? My vagina is reaching Sahara levels of dry.

He doesn't have stormy blue eyes or a soft scruffy beard or those little crinkles around his eyes. Maybe I shouldn't be comparing this guy to Brooks. Maybe it's not fair, but I guess this is where I'm at. He's not Brooks, so I'm not interested.

"Can you blame me? You're the prettiest girl I've ever seen, and it looks like you're here alone. I've gotta take a shot, right? I'm Kevin." He's leering at me, openly eyeing me like I'm a snack. It makes my skin crawl.

He flags the bartender to send over another round of drinks. Great. I open my mouth to say no thank you, but I'm interrupted by a deep voice coming from right behind me.

"She's not here alone."

I. Know. That. Voice. An excited shiver runs through my body, and my breath catches in my chest. I shouldn't feel relieved. I'm a grown ass woman and I can tell a dip shit like Kevin to shove off, but if Brooks wants to do it for me, I won't say no. I might even enjoy it a little bit.

I slowly spin on my bar stool and look up into the face of the man that I've been comparing Kevin to. I cross my legs and lean my elbows back on the bar, trying to look relaxed even though I feel anything but.

"What are you doing here, Brooks?"

Brooks looks me up and down hungrily. This gaze I don't mind. His eyes are burning with intensity as he puts his hands on the bar behind me, caging me. His face is inches from mine and I can feel his warm breath tickle my neck as he answers me.

"I'm here for you, obviously." His rough baritone sends waves of heat through my body and I clench my thighs together, wishing my body didn't react so strongly to his.

My eyes dart around the restaurant and to a wide-eyed Kevin still sitting next to me before landing back on the serious expression on Brooks' face.

"Hot and cold, much?" I ask as calmly as I can manage. My shallow rapid breathing betrays my voice though. He stares at me hard, blue eyes pinning me in place as he thinks for a second. His closeness has me on edge and I want him so badly. I'm equal parts terrified and hoping he's going to kiss me again. I lick my lips as I think about the way his lips felt on mine.

"Hey." Kevin seems to have collected some of his wits because he interrupts our staring contest. I don't know if he's a complete idiot or if he's had one too many drinks. Either way, he has the balls to grab Brooks by the arm. "I just bought her a drink, man. Wait your turn." The anger that flashes in Brooks' eyes would be frightening if it were directed at me. I scrunch up one eye, wincing. Bad move, Kevin.

Brooks slowly turns to look Kevin in the eye. His voice is deadly calm. "There will be no turns. She's with me. Now take your disgusting hand off me before I break your arm." If I was Kevin, I'd probably be peeing my pants right about now. He sure as fuck doesn't look very brave as he snatches his hand back and scoots to the other end of the bar like a kicked puppy.

Brooks turns his eyes back on mine, anger replaced with heat. He reaches one hand into his back pocket, still caging me in with his left arm, and leans even closer as he slaps some cash on the bar behind me. "We're leaving," he says before taking my elbow and pulling me off of my bar stool. He grabs my purse and leads me out of the restaurant.

His grip is firm but gentle. He's strong and I can tell he's being careful not to hurt me. Turns out I love the whole controlled power thing. I've never been turned on by the idea of an Alpha guy, but this is really doing it for me. Physically, at least. My brain is annoyed by my body's reaction to him, but he's like catnip for my lady parts.

It's cool and clear outside, the sidewalks quiet. Garland and Christmas lights are strung up all around the main square. It feels cheerful and romantic, but I'm too shell shocked by Brooks' chest thumping in the bar to enjoy it. I should drag my feet. I should pull away and go home alone. I should but I don't because I'm crazy turned on and I stupidly want to see where this is going.

"Can you get your big gorilla paw off of me and give back my stuff?"

Brooks pulls me close. I feel like he can see right through my skin to my heart frantically beating in my chest. He keeps a firm grip on my elbow and holds my purse out of reach as I snatch at it.

"What is going on with you?" he asks me quietly, his voice calm and in control. I glare at him. I don't want to fucking talk to him right now. "I'll give your purse back after you and I have a conversation. This," he swings my bag over our heads, "is insurance. You're not going to run off on me again. So I'll ask you one more time, what is going on with you?"

I debate trying to jump up and grab my purse, but I don't think I can reach it because he's so damn tall. If I was wearing my running shoes instead of these boots, I'd have a chance. Stupid, sexy footwear.

"Nothing is going on with me. I'm fine. I just want to go home."

Brooks eyes me hard. "Why are you acting like this?"

He's not angry, but he also won't let this go. He just keeps pushing and pushing and I feel like a volcano about to explode.

"Here's an easier one, why did you run off on me last night?" he shakes my elbow gently.

That insignificant movement shakes something loose in me and I finally reach the end of my cool. I've been stewing in a pot of sexual frustration, disappointment, hurt, and uncertainty for so long I can't contain myself anymore. I wrench my elbow out of his hand and ball my hands into fists.

"Because you didn't want me! Because I don't want to be kissed and then told that it was just a mistake!" My voice cracks. It's too much to admit, but I can't stop. "Because you looked at me like you regretted kissing me!"

Brooks' frustrated demeanor crumbles. He looks like I've struck him. "Is that really what you think?" He growls as he pulls my body flush against his, wrapping a warm arm around my back. My hands land on his chest, all hard planes and muscle. "I want you so fucking bad it hurts."

Startled, I lean back and look up into his eyes. "I... I..." I stammer like an idiot. I'm so confused, but hope replaces some of my anger. I must look like an idiot gawking at him like this but he doesn't seem to think so. Heat burns in his eyes and he looks at me like I'm the only woman on Earth.

"Jesus, Olive. I've been trying to go slow! I was trying to be patient." His voice is gravelly with emotion, and it makes me shiver. "I will never regret this."

He palms the back of my head and presses his lips to mine. He kisses me hungrily. Devouring my mouth, like he's starving for me. He pulls me tighter to his front, his thick arm wrapping me into him as his tongue brushes against the seam of my lips and lust ripples up my spine. I have never felt desire like this. I've never felt this desired, either.

Sliding my arms around his waist, I open my mouth and let him in. His kiss is an invasion, scorching in its intensity as his tongue slicks against mine, promising all the filthy things he can do with it. I'm lost in the current, moaning and arching into him as his fingers tunnel through my hair.

Brooks presses his forehead to mine, catching his breath. "I want you, Olive. Don't you dare doubt it for a second."

Chapter 22: Brooks

Olive's breath is ragged as she whispers the four best words I've ever heard anyone say. "I want you too."

I growl as I kiss her again. Her small hands roam over my arms and back as I hold her small frame flush against my body, her breasts pressing into my chest. I slick my tongue into her mouth, claiming her and she lets out a moan and hitches her leg over my hip. I'm palming her adorable curvy butt before I remember where we are. Not here. The possessive side of me doesn't want anyone to see Olive like this. Her touches, sultry looks, and little moans are all for me.

"Come home with me," I say breathlessly. I can't give her room to run right now. I need her next to me no matter what.

"My place is closer," she pants. She's right. Her bakery is only two blocks away. Might as well be two miles with her sweet vanilla scent hanging in the air and her taste on my lips.

"Still too far," I say before pulling her down the block to the alley where I parked my truck. Thank god it's close. I deposit her carefully inside before sliding in next to her. The second I get the door shut she clambers into my lap, mouth colliding with mine. The way she's straddling me causes her leather mini skirt to hitch up her tan thighs.

I'm a single minded man; in this moment, the only thing I care about is the pressure of her warm body as she grinds into my lap, kittenish mewls pouring into my greedy kisses. Gripping her hips, I pull her down hard, rubbing her panty covered pussy against the erection straining my pants.

"Oh, god," she pants against my mouth as her movements become frantic. "I need--" she breaks off with a little moan.

"You need more?" I taunt her sweetly as I slide her back a couple inches and press a finger against her clit through her panties. She cries out, eyelashes fluttering.

"Your panties are soaked," I purr into her ear. Slipping my free hand into the hair at the base of her neck, I wrap her locks around my fist and hold her face back from mine just an inch. Just far enough to watch her eyes as I slowly slip a finger under her panties and slide it along her drenched folds.

Her beautiful green eyes are hooded with lust as I inch my big finger into her needy pussy. It ripples and clenches around my digit and it's so tight even with just one finger that the thought of filling her with my cock has me almost coming in my pants like a teenager.

She licks her lips and her mouth falls partly open as she breathes my name. Those full lips would look so damn pretty sucking my cock.

"I can't stand to leave you wet and needy. I'm going to take the edge off right here. Then you're going to take me back to your place so I can lick your pussy until you come on my face over and over and over."

The dirtier I talk, the hotter and wetter she gets. I add a second finger and I have to tamp down a groan as her cunt clutches me greedily. She closes her eyes as I stroke inside her, but I need to see her when she falls over the edge. Using my grip on her ponytail, I angle her face closer to mine. "Look at me baby," I command. "I want to watch those pretty eyes while you come." I pull my hand free from her for just a second, licking my thumb, before thrusting back inside her, rubbing my thumb on her clit.

Olive starts to shake, chanting my name over and over on a soft moan like a prayer. And then it's "please Brooks, please Brooks, please." I'm fascinated, drowning in her eyes and lost to the world as I press my fingers hard against her g-spot, still thrusting and stroking her clit.

I see it in her eyes the second she lets go. Her pussy ripples and clenches around me as her eyes roll back in her head, a soundless scream on her lips. It's the most incredible thing I've ever seen. The moment of pure trust and ecstasy rolls over her and I'm so fucking grateful.

She comes back slowly and I hold her, her head pillowed on my chest. I slip my fingers free of her warm body and bring them to my lips. She looks up at me with a dazed and fascinated expression as I lick her off my fingers.

"Oh god," she whispers. "Why is that so fucking hot?"

I chuckle and rub my fingers over Olive's kiss-swollen lips. "Because you taste amazing?" Her little tongue darts out, and she nips the tip of my finger, pulling a groan from me. "I need more of you," I say. I kiss her again before sliding her back into the passenger seat, reaching around her languid body to buckle her in.

The drive to her apartment isn't long enough to warm up the truck. She looks half melted into the seat so I scoop her up and carry her to the side door that leads up to her apartment over the bakery. She bats at my chest. "I can walk. Put me down." She's laughing despite her protests. I set her down at the door so she can unlock it and let us in. She steps up the first step and turns to put her arms around my neck.

"I've never invited someone up here before."

Uncertainty lines her delicate features and all I want to do is make her smile. I nuzzle her neck and breathe in the sweet smell of her skin. "Well, that's not true. I know I've seen your sister go upstairs." I can feel her smile even before she chuckles.

"You know what I mean," she laughs.

Chapter 23: Olive

Brooks pulls his face back to look at mine, gently cupping my jaw with both of his enormous hands. "I do know what you mean," he says with a gentle smile. "Do you still want me to come up?" The porch light throws his face half in shadows, but I can still see those adorable crinkles around his eyes. Our bodies are pressed together, his erection grinding into the front of my pelvis and all I can think about is his promise to eat me until I come. Repeatedly.

"Oh, hell yes," I whisper before pulling his mouth back to mine. I'll never get enough of his kisses. Desire thrums through my body as Brooks grips my hips and backs me into the entryway. We climb the stairs. Sort of. Because I can't tear myself from his lips and his hands are all over my body. I fumble with his buttons as my cardigan falls away. His shirt goes the same way and my hands stroke up the planes of his chest, reveling in the sensations of his smooth skin, the hard muscles and the tickle of his chest hair. He's so fucking manly and I love it.

A warm hand wraps around my lower back, preventing me from falling backwards up the stairs and I giggle as he rips my shirt off over my head. I'm distracted by the sound of Brooks inhaling sharply. He leans back, looking me up and down, devouring me with his eyes. He cups my breast over the cream-colored lace of my bra, his thumb stroking my nipple.

"You are so goddamn beautiful," he whispers reverently. And the way he's looking at me, I believe him. Any insecurities I might have about my body be damned because this man doesn't seem to see them at all.

"I want you," I whisper back, arching into his touch. His hand on my ass lifts me against him and I wrap my legs around his waist, letting him carry me into the apartment. I'm so lost in the way he kisses me, tongue slicking against mine, claiming me and demanding more, I don't realize where we are until my back hits the bed. Brooks' enormous body hovers over mine and I wrap my legs around him even tighter, grinding against him, frantic with need. His control is iron clad though, because he unwraps me from his body, stealing the delicious friction. I moan at the loss, frustrated and needy.

Brooks chuckles gently, kissing his way down my jaw, the column of my throat and across my collar bone. He inches lower, his fingers leaving tantalizing trails of goosebumps for his mouth to follow. His hands cup my breasts, pinching and rolling my nipples through the lace until the tight little peaks are straining to escape.

Everything he does feels incredible, sparks of desire and pleasure slowly consuming me. When his warm mouth closes over one of the little buds and his teeth nip at me I nearly jump out of my skin, crying out for more and holding his head in my hands. My bra is off before I even realized he was unclasping the little front closure and his warm mouth closes around my other nipple. Cool air hits my damp areola causing the nipple to tighten to an almost painful degree. I'm so desperate my moans are taking on a plaintive note.

Brooks yanks the hem of my skirt up, pressing his palm against my mound and I cry out at the pressure and relief. "Yes-yes-yes," I hiss, rolling my hips to meet his blessed hand. He doesn't give me enough to come. I realize that he's doing it on purpose and I moan. It doesn't matter that he already made me come in his truck. I need it.

He sits up, pulling my skirt down my hips, taking my panties with it and I lift my butt, trying to help him as much as I can. As soon as he has me bare, Brooks' face is between my legs, my knees thrown over his shoulders. I lean up on my elbows because I want to see everything this man does. The scruff of his short beard tickles my inner thighs and I squirm as I realize he's got his nose in my trimmed curls and he's inhaling my scent. "You smell so good," he rumbles.

"Ohmygod, so dirty," I moan. I lift my hips, trying to get him closer.

"Not this pussy," Brooks replies with a smirk, his eyes blazing as he gives me a long slow lick. "Do you want to know what you taste like?" Another slow, tortuous lick. I'm panting, falling to pieces and all I can manage is a jerky little nod. "You taste like vanilla and spices and apples." He nuzzles my thigh, biting me gently. "You smell and taste like that all over, but you're especially delicious right here."

I never knew dirty talk was my thing, but damn, I am into this. Face back in my pussy, he licks my folds, pinpointing my clit and circling his tongue around it over and over until I'm shaking. I come, crying out, my thighs clenching around Brooks head in a death grip. He chuckles, pleased with himself as he eases back.

"You're so damn pretty when you come. Look how flushed you get." Brooks palms my stomach with one hand as his fingers stroke me, bringing me closer and closer to falling again. The pleasure and praise in his voice lights me up almost as much as his touch. "You like it when I talk dirty, don't you?" Brooks teases as he slides two fingers inside me.

I can't answer, too wrapped up in the sensation of his hands all over and inside me. I've already come twice but I still want more and I cry out as he pumps in and out of me. "I can tell you do pretty girl, here's the proof in your sopping wet pussy." His fingers make an obscene, wet sound as he fucks me with them. A fresh wave of lust tingles down my spine and Brooks chuckles. "So fucking wet and perfect," he whispers sinfully before putting his mouth back on my clit and sucking, drawing it into his lips. The sensation, combined with his fingers stroking inside me is too much, too intense, and I fall apart with a scream, his name on my lips.

Chapter 24: Brooks

I'm a goner. Nothing in the world will ever compare to the satisfaction of making Olive come all over my hands and face. In this moment, I know I've got to make her mine forever because there will never be another woman for me. The possessive feelings that have been growing inside of me for weeks crash over me and the need to claim her is overwhelming.

I shuck my pants and boxers, retrieving a condom and rolling it up my length. Climbing over Olive, I kiss my way up her stomach, and across the valley of her breasts. She lies languid beneath me, her hair a stunning dark cascade over the white pillow case. Her legs are sprawled open invitingly, and she wraps her arms around my ribs, pulling my weight over her. "I need you," she whispers. Her voice is a quiet plea.

My cock is hard and aching, and I rock against her, letting it slick through her wet folds but not entering her. The slick warmth is the single greatest torture I've ever experienced and from the mewling sound Olive makes she feels the same. "Like this?" I tease her. Olive growls a little moan at me and I chuckle, notching the broad head of my cock at her entrance and rubbing her there. "I'm trying to go easy on you," I tell her with a grin.

She scowls and throws her legs around my waist and digs her little heels into my backside. "Fuck that. I want all of you." I give her what we both need and slide into her, burying myself.

She's so tight it's a miracle I can even fit.

"So. Big," Olive gasps, holding me tight, digging her little fingertips into my biceps. I hold my breath and try not to move so I can regain some damn control. Her sweet pussy clenches around my length like a fist as she wiggles underneath me.

"Move. Oh please, god, move! I need it," Olive moans. Pressing my forehead to hers, I pump in and out, my breath rasping each time I sink back inside of her. Her back arches and she strains under me, making little sounds of pleasure as I run my free hand over her body. Every inch of her is silky smooth and I think I could happily spend a lifetime just tracing my fingertips along her curves. My fingers skate over ribs and around the outer curve of her breast, making her pussy grasp me even tighter. It feels like she's sucking me in deeper with each thrust.

"Jesus, you're so tight," I mutter.

Olive gives a breathless little laugh. "Yeah, well I didn't realize you were packing a monster dick. I might not have fought this so hard." Sitting back on my knees, I pull her up into my lap gripping her hips as she rocks back and forth, riding me, my dick buried so deep inside her I'm bottomed out and she's grinding her clit against the base of my cock.

She gyrates on me, panting, head thrown back in pleasure. Her breasts bounce and sway right in front of me. It's more than any man could resist. I draw her nipple into my mouth, sucking and biting until I feel her body tighten like a bow string. Her breath coming in little gasps and pants.

"That's it, come for me, baby," I demand. "I want to feel this pussy come all over my cock."

Her pussy clamps down around my cock as she comes, screaming my name. The flood of moisture and the tight clench of her pussy rippling with her orgasm is too much and I'm thrown over the edge with her, roaring my release. I swear to god, the world goes black. I can't see or hear anything. All I can feel is her lithe body, clutched tight in my arms. Her head resting on my shoulder and her long hair tickling my arm as we both try to breathe.

I recover first, gently untangling her legs from mine and heading to the bathroom. I throw the condom in the bathroom trash and then crawl back into bed, pulling Olive into my side. She rests her cheek on my shoulder, running warm little fingers through my chest hair. Reaching down to pull her leg over mine, I tuck her as close as I can, before stroking her hair.

The streetlight filtering in through the window highlights the curve of her breast, the dip of her waist and the swell of her hip. I trace my fingertips where the moonlight catches her soft skin, and my heart aches.

She's mine and I'll never let her go.

Chapter 25: Olive

Perfection. That's the only way to describe this moment. I'm completely sated. My body is a puddle of relaxation. Brooks made me come so hard and so many times I've basically lost all muscle control. I've had sex before but it sure as fuck never felt like this.

Honestly, I thought this kind of sexual chemistry was a myth. Or maybe I was just incapable of feeling it. Brooks just hit the reset button on my sexual expectations. He's surprisingly snuggly after, too. He's got me wrapped all around his body, caressing me sweetly and it's such a juxtaposition to the raunchy, hair pulling, public finger fucking, dirty talking sex god he was just minutes ago. I love both sides of him though. Fuck. Let's just shove that thought really, really deep down.

I give a little shiver as Brooks traces my hip bone and kisses my temple. "You ok?" he asks, peering down at me. "You're thinking too hard. Maybe I need to make you come again," he teases.

I chuckle. "Please no, I think I might die if I come again." I attempt to erase any worry from my face. I just want to enjoy this. "Do you want to stay?" It comes out more hesitant than I mean it too. Brooks studies my face with a boyish smile, the one he only seems to give me.

"Hell yes," he says before kissing me. Relief washes over me. I didn't realize how afraid I was that he would want to leave until now.

"Um, ok. I mean, good. That's good." I suddenly feel so shy. I know it's ridiculous because he was balls deep inside of me less than five minutes ago.

I start to get up to go clean myself up, but he pulls me back down on top of him.

"Where are you running off to?" he asks, pulling my hair to one side and nuzzling my neck.

"I was just going to brush my teeth and kind of clean all this up," I reply and gesture at my whole body with more bravado than I really feel. The truth is I feel so vulnerable that I just wanted to hide in the bathroom for a minute and collect myself.

"Mm hm…" he hums into my neck. "But you smell like me, and like sex, and maybe I like you just a little dirty." He gives me a roguish smile before licking the shell of my ear and making me giggle. When he nips at the sensitive lobe, I get wet all over again. That should not feel as good as it does.

"If you let me get cleaned up, then you can make me dirty all over again," I try to reason with him.

"How about we get cleaned up together and in the morning I'll make you breakfast and get you nice and dirty before we have to work?" Brooks negotiates like a champ because I sure as hell can't turn down an offer that good. I nod and lead him to the bathroom.

I pull out a new toothbrush for him while he turns the water on in the shower for us. I can't help admiring his tight butt as he leans into the shower, testing the water. I have an internal debate over whether to smack his ass but he catches me staring before I can decide and looks my very naked body up and down with burning approval before pulling me into him and kissing me deeply.

The bathroom is steamy by the time we get into the shower. Objectively, I always knew it wasn't a huge shower, but I never realized how small it was until this enormous man tried to stand under the shower head. He has to stoop to get the water to spray the top of his head and the sight makes me giggle. Brooks grins and pulls me into him, making water spray all over my face. I sputter as he apologizes and wipes the water away from my eyes. It's such a ridiculous and tender moment. I kind of want to stand like this all night.

Brooks is dead set on cleaning me within an inch of my life though. He pours way too much body wash out on my loofah and insists on rubbing me down all over before rinsing me off. He finally lets me have control of the loofah and I take my time, letting the soapy water run down his abs in little rivulets. By the time I'm done with his arms and chest, his dick is hard as a rock and pointing straight up at me. It really is a monster of a dick. I've never seen one so big before and I'm fascinated. Gently, I wrap my hand around it and give him a slow stroke.

Brooks moans my name and leans his head back against the tile, watching me with his stormy eyes. "You were just begging me to stop making you come but if you keep touching me like that, I won't be able to help myself…"

I give him a coy smile. "I didn't really beg you to stop." I can't help teasing him with a long firm stroke. The tenderness in Brooks' eyes melts into smoldering intensity as he grips my hips and spins me around. He wraps his arms around me, pressing his front into my back, his hard cock sliding against the curve of my butt as his warm body slicks against mine.

"Mouthy girl," Brooks whispers into my ear before nipping his way down my neck. Oh god, did I think I was done with him for the night? I might have been sated twenty minutes ago but Brooks' mouth is lighting my body up all over again. I rock my ass back against him. I feel achingly empty. "Do you have any condoms in here?" He asks as he bites my neck gently.

"Top left drawer, I think." He leans out of the shower and roots around in the drawer, just within reach. He comes up with a foil packet and checks the date.

"Still good," he grins at me. "Lucky me."

He presses my body forward so my hands and cheek press against the cool tile. Tension curls in my belly as I hear him rip the package open and sheath himself. He hooks an arm under my right knee, opening me up and sliding home in one brutal thrust. The sudden sensation of being so full erases the aching need and I cry out, gasping against the tile. He swears under his breath, but I don't catch all of it as I lose myself in him.

Brooks wraps his enormous forearm across my chest, holding me tight and arching my body like a bow, finely tuned and ready to fire. He's so close, his breath ragged in my ear as he fills me over and over. There's a slight shift in angles and then, without warning, my orgasm overtakes me with a muffled scream.

Brooks shudders his release, holding me as we sag against the shower wall together.

Chapter 26: Brooks

Olive has a satisfied look on her face as she turns and grins up at me. I wrap her in my arms, skin slippery as I cradle her to my chest. She hums a carefree sound. I'd like nothing more than to stay like this forever. Practicality is against me though because I can tell the hot water is running out.

"Holy hell," I mutter. I take a minute to catch my breath, throwing the condom in the trash and rinsing off before shutting off the water. Olive lets me wrap her in a towel and eyes me appreciatively as I wrap one around my own waist. We dry ourselves off as best we can and fall into bed, naked and exhausted.

"I wish we didn't have to work tomorrow," she pretends to pout, sticking out her full bottom lip and looking up at me through her thick eyelashes. I run the pad of my thumb over her pout and draw her lip down.

"I fucking love this mouth," I whisper, cupping the back of her neck and kissing her gently. I pull her against my chest, as close as I can get her, with her head tucked under my chin. I drift off, stroking her hair and feeling deeply content.

I wake up early the next morning, sunrise still hours away. Olive has her leg thrown over my hips, and her head pillowed on my shoulder. The sheet has slipped down, so it barely covers her hips.

Her bare breasts are pressed against my ribs and I'm already hard and aching for her. I press my nose into the tousle of her hair and inhale. She smells so fucking good.

"Are you sniffing me?" she asks sleepily. She hasn't moved a muscle and if not for her question she could still be sleeping.

I huff her hair even harder. "I am definitely sniffing you."

"Weirdo," she chuckles, her eyes still closed as I run my hand up and down her bare spine. She shivers happily and burrows in even closer to my side. "Mmm… that feels good," she murmurs.

Her plush lips are curled up in a soft smile and she still hasn't opened her eyes.

"Look at me, baby."

She peeks at me through one eyelid. "But if I open my eyes, then I have to start my day, and I just want to lay here like this."

I gently roll her to her back and drink up the sight of her. She's all smooth caramel skin, curves and dips. I'm going to lick every inch of her.

"Keep your eyes closed then," I whisper. Starting at the graceful curve where her throat and shoulder meet, I lick and kiss and nip my way down her body, paying extra attention to the spots that make her squeal and sigh and moan.

Olive dutifully keeps her eyes closed, even when I find the ticklish spot on the inside of her thigh. Her giggles turn to sweet sighs as I settle myself between her thighs and lick her until she comes hard. Twice.

Chapter 27: Brooks

We stay in bed so long that, in the end, there's no time for food at all. We rush around getting dressed, but I can't help stealing touches and glances as we move around each other. Olive walks me to the apartment door and I wrap my arms around her, holding her close and kissing her until I'm ready to say fuck it all and let the world burn down around us.

Olive pulls away with a moan and a resigned look on her face. Her lips are swollen, and she still looks slightly rumpled. It's sexy as hell.

"Rain check on breakfast?" she asks with a rueful smile.

"Let me make you dinner tonight? I mean, I didn't go to culinary school or anything, but I can cook a little. I'll pick you up at 5?" My heart is thumping erratically, afraid she will say no. Or, even worse, she intended this to be a one-time thing.

Not that it matters because I'll just convince her to see me again, anyway. Now that I've had a night with Olive, I don't plan on spending another one alone as long as I live.

But my worries are for nothing because she gives me a grin and nods. I kiss her again and start down the stairs only to find the scattered clothing I ripped off of Olive as we came up last night.

She giggles as I collect her blouse and sweater and turn back up to return them.

"Oh lord, just toss those up here," she calls down. I ball the smooth shirt up inside the sweater thing and chuck it up to her. She's blushing and my cheeks hurt from smiling so much. I can't remember the last time I felt so light. Olive blows me a kiss and I give her a wink.

"See you in a bit," I promise.

Somehow, I sneak out to my truck without any of Olive's employees or her sister catching me. I'd be perfectly happy if everyone knew where I spent the night, but Olive pointed out how unprofessional it would be for both of us. I grudgingly agreed, although I sincerely doubt Luis missed my truck sitting in the small lot overnight.

I hope he tells everyone.

I have to speed home to get fresh clothes, but I make a quick stop at the grocery store for dinner supplies. I throw everything together, tidy up my house a little and I'm still back at the bakery before most of my guys show up for work.

With a grin, I spring up the front steps and through the front door, sliding into the line to order my coffee and muffin. The bakery is crowded, breakfast pastries flying out the door. Olive is great at this.

My admiration is interrupted by the sight of my favorite woman emerging from the kitchen, carrying a sheet tray loaded up with muffins and pastries to refill the dwindling supply in the display case. She balances the tray in one hand, restocking the display with her other. I can tell the moment she sees me in line because she blushes and drops a croissant. She recovers with a grin and waves me out of the line, gesturing to meet her at the pick up area on the other end.

By the time I squeeze out of line and make it down there, Olive is waiting for me with a large cup of coffee and a little box. My name is scrawled across the top and when I peek inside there are two of my favorite lemon poppyseed muffins nestled into some bakery tissue.

She had this ready for me. My chest squeezes a little because she clearly went out of her way to package these up and set them aside. She's just so goddamn thoughtful. I want to kiss her, but she just gives me a wink and darts away.

"You okay, boss?" a voice chuckles behind me.

"Huh?" I turn and see Charlie grinning at me. How long was I standing here like a lovesick idiot?

He looks smug and a little too knowing. "Oh, nothing. I was just worried about the way you were staring longingly at that doorway."

"Oh fuck off, Charles," I mutter at him. He just laughs. I'm not sharing my muffins with him.

Chapter 28: Olive

My day drags by. I try not to watch Brooks out the window, but I can't help myself. I'm not as sneaky as I should be, and Lilah catches me more than once. She came in this afternoon after another long night at the bar. I'm always happy to have her here. It feels less like work and more like hanging out, even if I still have a ton to finish.

I'm shaping tart shells and most definitely not checking out Brooks' tight butt as he talks to one of his guys. Over and over, my mind replays the way he pulled me into his lap and made me come in the front seat of his truck last night. I'm so lost in my thoughts that I didn't even realize Lilah had sidled up next to me.

"Whatcha lookin' at?" She nudges me in the side with her elbow, and I let out a surprised shriek.

"Nothing," I reply, guiltily. Terrible recovery.

"Oh really? So you were mangling the innocent tart shell for no reason?" Lilah laughs.

Looking down at my hands I realize I've been pressing the same piece of dough down into the tart shell and it is, in fact, completely trashed. "Oh. I'm a little out of it."

"Mm-hm. 'Out of it' is one way to put it." She makes sarcastic air quotes. "You've been staring at Mr. Contractor like you want to eat him all day."

I ignore my sister and toss the ruined tart shell in the trash, moving on to a new one. I can, quite literally, shape tart shells with my eyes closed. I haven't had to redo a tart shell in years, but today I am hopeless.

"You know, a little birdie told me you were having drinks with Brooks last night."

"What?" I gasp. "Who told you that? We weren't having drinks. He showed up at the bar after Chelsea had to cancel. Some dip was hitting on me and Brooks just charged in and demanded I leave with him. I don't even know how he knew I was there…" It just occurred to me that I never asked how he found me.

Lilah is trying to keep a straight face, but she's doing a terrible job suppressing her self-satisfied smirk. "So you left with him? Where exactly did you go?"

My mouth hangs open. "It was you! You told him where I was?"

Lilah puts on an indignant face. "I most certainly did not!" I know my sister. She most certainly did. And I know just how to make her admit it. I cross my arms and stare at her stone faced, completely silent. She lasts all of twenty seconds before she cracks. "But I might have mentioned where you were going to Luis. Loudly."

"Judas," I mutter.

She has the decency to look guilty as she picks up a piece of dough and starts shaping tarts with me. "You didn't answer me. Where did you and Brooks go after Chelsea's fender bender?"

I almost drop the tart ring on the floor, suspicions swirling.

"Holy shit. How much of yesterday did you plan?! Did you get Chelsea and Sally both in on it?"

Lilah holds up her hands and giggles nervously. "It's not like I had some master scheme or anything! Sally wasn't in on it. That was just super good luck. She texted me after she sent you to the spa. She was worried about you. And after I talked to Brooks yesterday, well, he was desperate to talk to you. I knew where you were going to be… and once I told Chelsea what was going on, she was happy to excuse herself and let Brooks take his shot."

I can't believe this. I should be livid… but given the way it worked out, how can I be? Maybe I needed a little push in the right direction. Of course my sister went a little nuts, but whatever.

"Did Chelsea even get rear-ended?"

"Nope. She was actually at the coffee shop two doors down from the restaurant in case it all blew up and you were upset."

I blanch. "The coffee shop next to the alley?"

Lilah gives me a weird look, taking a second to think about the layout of the streets. "Yeah, I guess it is next to an alley, why?"

I do not recover well. "Um, it's nothing. We just kind of made out in the alley." I mumble and blush, remembering the extremely filthy things we did in Brooks' truck. I hope to god Chelsea kept her butt in the coffee shop.

Lilah laughs, patting my red cheek. "That's a lot of blushing for 'just kinda made out.'" She wiggles her fingers in air quotes as she teases me. "Luis says his truck was here overnight. Tell me you didn't bring him back here to just 'kinda make out.'"

"There are an egregious amount of air quotes being used in this conversation," I point out.

"Don't change the subject! I'll just keep going with the 'air quotes' until you fill me in."

"God, you're so annoying," I say and smack her hands out of the air. "Finish these tarts with me. I did bring him back to the apartment. We did a little more than making out but I'm not giving you specific details so get your mind out of the gutter."

"Hussy!" She cackles. "You bumped uglies!"

"Shhh! Don't be a child!" I hiss back at my sister. She looks like she's positively gloating. My eyes dart out the window and my heart skips a beat to see Brooks looking back at me from the outside lot. He grins and winks at me, and I grin back.

Lilah just looks smug. "So, are you guys, like, together now?"

"No. Yes. Maybe. I don't know. I think so? We didn't actually talk much." My face is blazing now. "He asked if I would eat dinner at his house tonight though." I bite my lip, suddenly unsure. We really didn't talk about this beyond "I want you."

Lilah grins at me. "Maybe you should try talking to him during dinner then. Wait to jump his bones until after you have a conversation."

***

I work through lunch and by the time four o'clock rolls around I'm basically stewing in my own nerves and anxiety. The only thing saving me from going absolutely insane is the mountain of work I need to finish. Inventory, prep lists, placing orders, and payroll keep me running all day.

Lilah says I should stop worrying and just talk to Brooks. She's right, of course, but it doesn't stop my mind from running wild.

I know he said he would never regret "this" and then kissed me, but we had like zero conversation beyond that. We just went from zero to sixty in the hook up department. To me, it felt like we were getting together, but what if that's not what Brooks meant? In my experience, men don't stick around. I want to believe that Brooks is better than that. I do believe it. But it's still a hard thing for me to wrap my head around.

"Stop stewing!" Lilah scolds as she walks by carrying a tray of hot chocolate chip cookies. I huff at her, but she's right. I've been nervously chewing my lip so much that I need to find some chapstick. I quickly finish cleaning up my station and check in with my prep staff.

Everything is running smoothly, even with all the extra Christmas orders, so I run upstairs to shower and get cleaned up for dinner with Brooks. I manage to shave my legs, blow dry my hair and throw on some mascara and chapstick in record time, but standing in front of my closet, I'm stumped.

What exactly does a girl wear for a first date with a man she's already slept with? Considering that I really need to talk to Brooks before anything else happens, maybe I should wear Granny panties and a bunch of layers? I wonder if that would keep things PG? Pfft. I doubt it.

I'm still in my towel when my phone rings. Davidson Construction is calling. Maybe I should change the ID in my phone, I laugh to myself before answering.

"Hey."

"Hey yourself," Brooks replies. I can hear the grin in his voice. "I'm on my way. I'll be there in five minutes."

I do a double take and look at the clock. "You're early!" I accuse. "It's only 4:40 and I'm not ready yet."

"Well then, you better hurry your cute butt up then."

"I'm still in a towel!"

"Oh good, I'll come up."

"No you will not! I haven't eaten all day and if you come up here, I won't get to eat for hours."

Brooks laughs. "I do plan on feeding you…"

"Good. I'll be down in five," I say before hanging up.

Taking a deep breath, I grab a black wrap dress and my sexiest set of black mesh lingerie. I dress at warp speed and toss on my favorite black booties before checking myself in a mirror. My boobs look awesome in this dress so I'm going with it, but I double knot the bow just in case.

By the time I get my coat on and run downstairs, Brooks is out of his truck and leaning on the back end of the bed. He's got one hand in his pocket and is typing something on his phone with the other. He looks up when I walk out the door, gives me a big grin, and pockets his phone. He's wearing gray pants that accentuate his muscular thighs and his pale blue dress shirt fits like a sexy as hell glove. He dressed up, I realize. For me. It's a panty dropping look.

As soon as I get within arms reach of Brooks, he pulls me into him, wrapping me up in his arms. I should be worried our employees are going to see us, but I just can't find it in myself to care. His woodsy scent warms me all the way through.

"You look good enough to eat," I tell him, running my fingers along the buttons of his shirt.

Brooks cups my cheek in his hand, kissing me sweetly before running his mouth along my jaw and murmuring, "So do you." My eyes close at his touch. I love that this is all it takes to make me completely melt into him. Forget talking, all I want in the world is to wrap myself around his body and see how many times we can make each other come.

Thank god Brooks is more responsible than me. He pulls back and walks me to the passenger seat with his hand on my lower back. I feel like a child scrambling up into his monster of a truck, but I make it into the seat with my dignity relatively intact. "Maybe you can buy me a step stool or something," I tease Brooks.

"I could, but I have to admit I like watching your little butt hop up there," he replies with a cocky grin. God, everything he does is sexy. I purse my lips and pretend to look annoyed, but I'm not fooling anyone.

I was going to try to wait until after dinner to talk to Brooks, but I'm so twisted up inside. My nerves have me fidgeting as we drive down the road away from my bakery. I know he can tell something is up because he gently presses down on my bouncing knee. A minute later he takes my tapping fingers in his hand.

I try to relax but my anxiety is still spilling over the level that I can physically contain. I can't help fidgeting. I just need an outlet for my nerves. When I still can't hold still, Brooks pulls his truck off the road and parks it in the empty lot of a shuttered farm stand. He gives me a worried look, his eyes piercing.

"Too much coffee today?" he asks.

After stressing about this all day, I know I need to suck it up and get this over with. It's better to know now if this is just a casual thing, right? What I can't deal with is the not knowing.

"I might have had one too many cups of coffee but that's not it. I'm just really not good with ambiguity."

"What's ambiguous?" Brooks looks confused. And sexy. So sexy.

I start to explain, but I snap my mouth shut. Suddenly I don't want to bring this up. I just want to enjoy my time with him and not risk upsetting whatever this thing is. What happens if he's not ready to define this? Or worse, what if he confirms the worst things I've been thinking? That maybe this is just a quick fling. An itch to scratch. What if he just enjoys the chase? I already slept with him. Did that start a timer on his interest in me?

I don't have to say a thing though because Brooks must see what I'm thinking written all over my face. His confusion melts into a wide, heartbreaking smile, and he brushes my hair behind my ear. His fingertips trace their way down my neck, stroking the length of my arm. He takes my wrist in his hand, rubbing his thumb over the sensitive skin and a shiver runs through me.

"Oh Sugar. There's no ambiguity here. I'm going to be greedy with you for as long as you'll let me. This is new and we can see how it goes but I'm telling you right now, I'm keeping you for myself." His grip tightens on my wrist as he leans in and trails kisses along my jaw.

I think I've forgotten how to breathe properly. Brooks pulls me sideways across his lap, holding my face in one of his big calloused hands. The steering wheel is digging into my hip, but I don't care. My heart is racing as we kiss. I want more of him, but my stomach growls loud enough to interrupt us.

"Jesus, I need to feed you," Brooks laughs. He slides me back over into my seat and waits for me to buckle up before pulling back out onto the road.

"Keep kissing me like that and I might let you keep me," I tell him, heart fluttering. "I kind of like you." He lifts my hand to his lips, kissing my knuckles and giving me a heartbreaking smile.

I've always protected myself, careful not to let anyone close enough to hurt me. No one has ever been worth the risk before. This feels a lot like jumping off a bridge with just a bungee cord between my heart and the rocks below.

I didn't mean to let Brooks in, but he busted the damn door off the hinges and got in any way. Please don't break my heart, I silently pray.

Chapter 29: Brooks

After weeks of pushing and seemingly getting nowhere with Olive, I'm relieved to have her tucked up in my truck, taking her home with me. She looks so good like this. The sun streaming in behind her, making her hair shine as she smiles at me. She wears her emotions all over her face and I can see how much trust it's taking for her to let me in. She's being brave and I swear to god, I'll never give her a reason to be sorry she trusted me.

As we drive south to my house, I'm getting more and more nervous. Thirty-three years old and I've never brought a woman home like this. I've dated here and there, but never anything serious. I never thought I had the time but, in reality, I never made the time. I sat down and looked at my schedule today, rearranging things to make sure I had time to see Olive every day after she finished at the bakery.

It wasn't even hard. I've always hired enough help as the company grew. I make sure I take care of my employees and get as little turnover as possible. It was just good business sense in the past, but now it's going to free me up to spend as much time with Olive as possible.

I drive up the narrow lane to my house and I can't help eyeing Olive, waiting for her reaction. I bought the land three years ago and built the house myself. It's a modern two-story with an open floor plan and the most amazing view out over a neighboring vineyard. I put in a huge master suite, opening onto a balcony overlooking the natural stone pool.

It's everything I ever wanted in a house, but after seeing Olive's little apartment with its eclectic styling, I'm afraid she's going to hate it. I'd rather squash into the little studio above the bakery with her than live out here alone. Maybe I can convince her to help me redecorate it. Or I can sell it. Whatever she wants.

The road bends, and my house comes into view behind a stand of oak trees.

"Holy shit!" Olive's pretty mouth hangs open in shock and she looks back at me before gaping at the house again. I've been in this business long enough to know that's a good reaction and my nerves ease. A little.

Parking the car in the driveway, I'm out of the truck before Olive is even unbuckled. She lets me help her down, her warm hand clasped in mine and just that contact is enough to set my heart thumping in my chest.

"What do you think?" I ask, keeping my eyes on her as she looks up at the house.

She examines the house for a moment and then turns to me with squinted eyes, trying to contain a smile. "What I want to know, is why the hell would we stay at my crappy apartment last night when you've been sitting on this beast?"

Chuckling, I wrap an arm around her shoulder and pull her close to my side. "Because your apartment was closer and you couldn't wait to sit on my beast."

Olive lets out a short laugh and slaps my chest. "I'd be pissed at you for talking to me like that if it weren't true. Show me around, feed me, and then we can see about that beast of yours." Pleasure rumbles through me at the thought, but I stuff the desire down and lead her around to the front door.

She's a toucher, I realize. I see a lot of people explore new spaces after we build them. Most people are content to look, but some have to touch everything. Olive can't seem to help herself as she walks into my house. Her fingers graze the wall, flit over my lamp, and run along the back of my couch.

She's mesmerizing. Leaning back against the door, watching her, it's a moment I know I'm going to remember for the rest of my life.

This thing between us has been stirring since the moment she opened the hotel door, green eyes shining. I've already claimed her as mine. Now that I finally have her here, I know I won't be able to let her go back to her apartment. She would make this place feel like a real home and I'll fight to keep her here.

Olive grins at me from the couch. "What's that look for?"

"Nothing. You just make me happy," I tell her, moving to take her hand and pull her up. "Let me feed you and then I'll give you a tour." The whole house smells like the pot roast I put in the crock pot this morning and it's making my stomach rumble.

"God, this kitchen!" Olive exclaims. She admires my stovetop before spotting the crock pot with the pot roast bubbling away and laughs. "That explains the delicious smell. Did you really come home and put dinner in the crock pot for me this morning?"

"I promised to feed you and this is one of the few things I can make without fail." I grin at her wide eyed look and pull a loaf of bread out of its Olive Branch Bakery bag. "Plus I bought a loaf of rosemary sourdough from this really amazing bakery."

"Jesus, that's simultaneously the cutest and sexiest thing you've ever said." Her dress swishes around her hips as she walks around the kitchen, inspecting my appliances. It is very distracting. I pull out a chair at the table and gesture for Olive to have a seat. I just need her to hold still for a minute or I'm not going to make it through dinner.

Unfortunately, I'm no less distracted by a sitting Olive than I was a swishing one. Her wrap dress hugs her curves and when she sits, crossing one leg over the other, the skirt of her dress slips to the side, exposing the smooth caramel of her knees and tantalizing stretches of thigh.

She catches me staring and gives me a downright smug smile. The little minx did it on purpose! Oh, she's going to get it. Growling, I remind myself I promised to feed her.

"Tell me about your house. I'm curious." Olive bounces one foot absentmindedly while she watches me slice the bread.

"What do you want to know?"

"Well… when did you buy it, I guess?" She props her chin on her hand, waiting for me to answer her.

"I built it, actually. It's how I met Della."

"No way! She was your architect?"

"Yeah. She did a great job too."

"I'm kind of pissed she kept you a secret for so long," Olive squints at me.

I set a plate in front of Olive, piled high with meat, potatoes, and carrots smothered in gravy. I've had enough lunches with Olive to know that she can really eat. I put my plate in front of the chair next to hers and sit down.

"To be fair, Della and her husband offered to set me up a couple of times over the last few years and I refused. I don't date… well, I *didn't* date, anyway." She's still way too far away, so I hook my foot around the leg of her chair and pull her closer.

Olive gives me a huge smile. "Is that what this is? Are we dating?"

I'm not sure how to answer that. "Dating seems to imply that this is a trial run. 'Dating' doesn't seem permanent enough of a word." I stroke my fingertips down the column of her neck, watching the heat flare in her eyes.

Olive blushes. "This is new for me too, but I get it. I haven't dated anyone in a very long time."

"I like that I'm the exception and you're not just dating me for my money and awesome house," I joke.

111

Olive throws her head back and laughs. "Bitch please, I'm independently wealthy."

"Oh yeah? I didn't realize the baking business was so lucrative."

"Oh it definitely isn't. I mean, the bakery is in the black, and financially stable but I had help buying it. My Grandpa left my siblings and I trust funds before he died. I don't like to tell people. They tend to write off all the hard work I put into school and running my bakery."

I'm surprised. I guess I might have the same expectations as other people when it comes to trust fund kids. "At the risk of sounding like a dick, I wouldn't have expected someone who works as hard as you do to have money like that. And your siblings all work full time too?"

Far from looking offended, Olive gives me a proud smile. "Julia is in school full time finishing her nursing degree but the rest of us work. Grandpa had a great work ethic. Gran too."

"Don't get me wrong, we had a huge hand up. We all had separate educational trusts. Our full trusts were released to us when we turned 23 on the condition that we used our trusts to further our educations. We have a lot of freedom to pursue the careers we want without having to worry about failing and ending up broke."

"My brothers both got degrees in engineering but love cars so they used some of their trust to start an auto repair shop. Lilah has a degree in marketing with a minor in event planning. She barely touches her trust though. I think she feels icky about them."

I give her a confused look. "Why?"

Scrunching up my face, I warn Brooks, "It's not a very nice story."

I stroke my hand up and down her arm, trying to reassure her. "I want to hear it. I want to know everything about you, even the not so nice stuff."

Breaking off a piece of bread and swirling it around her plate, she sighs. "Ok. You asked for it. Keep in mind, most of this I've picked up from Gran but I've had to pull it out of her piece by piece."

"The trust funds are the reason our dad left us. Mom married him fresh out of high school. She was young and crazy in love and overlooked some of his less desirable traits. Like the drinking and how interested he was in Grandpa's money."

"Grandpa inherited a couple hundred thousand dollars from his Grandfather. He invested in properties all over California just in time for the housing boom. He built a small empire in the 60s and 70s before changing track and investing in a couple of Silicon Valley start-ups. It paid off big time."

Olive is quiet for a second. "This part sucks," she says as she fiddles with her fork.

"We can talk about it another time if you'd rather," I tell her.

She shakes her head. "No, it's better to just tell you now."

Chapter 30: Olive

I hate telling this story. Truthfully, I've only told a handful of people everything. It's depressing and I hate it when people feel sorry for me. I'll have to tell him sometime though and we're already here so I might as well push through.

"My dad married my mom expecting to work for my Grandpa. He just wanted to ride his coattails, really. He had no work ethic, no higher education, and he drank too much. He used to get pissed that Grandpa didn't do more for us, when in reality, Grandpa bought their house and paid most of the bills."

Brooks has a stormy expression on his face, but he's holding my hand and stroking the back of my knuckles soothingly.

"Once Mom got pregnant with me and Asher, she had to quit her job. They had all five of us in less than seven years. My mom always wanted a big family and Dad knew Grandpa would pay for anything we needed so he went along with it. He was always a bit of a jerk but we didn't spend much time with him so it wasn't that bad."

"When I was six, Mom went to lunch with Grandpa. She left us with the next-door neighbors. She was driving, and another driver ran a red light. Mom and Grandpa both died at the scene. A couple weeks later, Dad dropped us off with Gran. He told us he would be back in a couple hours and sent us inside."

"He argued with Gran outside and then drove off and we never saw him again. For years, she told us he went to work on an oil rig in the Gulf of

Mexico and couldn't take us with him. But he never called and never came back. I was a teenager when she finally admitted he abandoned us and never intended to come back. It was all because he didn't feel like he got his share of the money."

"Grandpa left almost all of his money to Gran and to his grandchildren in trust funds. He left $50,000 to my dad as a show of goodwill. He set the trusts up so that our father could never touch a dime of our money unless we chose to give it to him, which we could only do after we turned twenty-three and had pursued higher education."

"Dad tried to convince Gran to change the terms of the trust funds and even demanded she give him a portion of the money Grandpa left for her. When she refused, he told her that if she wouldn't give him access to our money, then we were her problem. She gladly invited him to fuck off and leave us with her. And he did."

Brooks is shaking with anger. His lips are a tight line in his handsome face. "What kind of man could do that?"

I shrug. "He wasn't much of a man. We were better off though. I'm honestly glad he left. Without Mom to love us, we would have grown up miserable with him. In the weeks after Mom died, he turned into a monster. I don't know if she had been protecting us or if he was just really messed up about her death, but once she was gone he started yelling, calling us mistakes and accidents. He even hit Asher once."

Brooks sucks in a breath, and he's clenching his fists on the table. Prying his fingers with mine, I get him to relax his hands. Looking down at our intertwined fingers, I smile. His hands are huge, and they swallow mine up.

"I didn't tell you this to make you upset. I just want you to understand how much better things were with Gran. The first night at her house was the first peaceful night we had since we lost Mom. Asher and I remember Gran putting on cartoons and giving us hot cocoa while she held Julia and made us dinner. Baked chicken with green beans and crinkle fries."

Taking a deep breath, I go on. "The other reason I'm telling you this is so you understand why I'm sensitive about certain things. Like feeling unwanted or a mistake."

Brooks scrubs a hand over his jaw. He almost looks shell shocked. He doesn't say anything for a second and I can just see the wheels turning in his head. I give him some time. He probably needs it because I just unloaded a pile of personal shit on him.

Finally he looks at me. "I swear, if I ever get my hands on him he will be sorry for what he put you through. And I'm sorry if I ever made you feel unwanted. Jesus. I came really close to completely fucking this up, didn't I?"

I hold my fingers up to say "a little."

Brooks lets out a rueful laugh before leaning in to kiss me gently. "In that case, thank you for giving me a second chance." He winces. "And a third. I promise you I won't need another one." Brooks hauls me into his lap, circling his arms around my waist before pulling my plate closer.

"What are you doing?" I ask him with a giggle.

"You were too far away, and you looked too sad. I can't stand it when you look sad," he says as he nuzzles my neck. The soft bristles of his beard brush along my collar bone. "Thank you," he says in a gruff voice.

"For what?" I ask him, stroking my hand over his chest.

Brooks places a hand on the side of my neck and strokes my cheek with his thumb. "For trusting me. For letting me in like this. You have a beautiful heart and I'm grateful I get to see it."

Chapter 31: Olive

Brooks holds me in his lap while we finish dinner. I try to get up once, but he just growls and holds me tighter. I like it enough to try it three more times. The conversation turns lighter and we sit like that for ages talking about our favorite movies, bakery and construction disasters, and dream vacations.

Brooks has a hand on my thigh while we talk, his thumb running up and down the smooth slip of my dress. It started as a soothing touch but the longer he does it, the more it turns me on. There's something possessive about the way he touches me, like he can't stand to keep his hands to himself.

There's a lull in the conversation as we both sip from our wine glasses and Brooks' hand strays a little higher on my thigh. He looks lost in thought, but his lips are pulling up on one side in a half smile. It's the smirk he wears when he's feeling satisfied with himself or when he knows something is turning me on. It's the look he wears when he's just made me come. The thought has me pressing my thighs together a little harder.

"What are you thinking about right now?" I ask him. "You look like you're thinking dirty thoughts," I tease him.

He chuckles darkly. "I am."

A curl of desire twists in my abdomen and I can't help wiggling a little in his lap. "About me? I want to hear them."

He takes a long slow sip of wine before setting the glass down and stroking his fingertips up and down my thigh. "I was thinking about the way your skin feels under this thin little dress. I was remembering how good these long legs of yours felt wrapped around me when I was deep in you last night."

"Oh," my breath catches and I can feel my cheeks heat as I mentally replay the same thing.

Brooks runs a finger over my parted lips and gently grips the back of my neck with the other hand. "You look scandalized but I know you like it when I talk dirty to you."

"I do," I whisper. I really, really like it. The more he talks and the more possessive he is, the wetter my panties get. I'm seriously in danger of leaving a wet spot on his lap at this point.

As if he knows exactly what I'm thinking, he slides a rough palm up my thigh, slowly. Painfully slowly. Brooks nuzzles my ear, speaking low. "I think you like it when I put you in my lap and take control. How wet does your pussy get when I talk dirty to you? If I slipped my hand up your dress and under your panties, what would I find?"

I try to bite back a moan, but I'm not very successful. His fingertips dance over my thigh, confident and teasing. "You're so soft here," he murmurs. "I could touch you like this until you're aching for more. I could make you beg for my cock. Make you wild and needy for it."

His hand inches higher and his fingers graze the lace panel of my panties, barely touching me, teasing me, as I moan into the corded muscles of his neck. I rock on his lap, and he lets out a low groan. I hiss in a breath as I feel his hard length grind against me. I wiggle in his lap, loving the feel of his arousal. The physical evidence that he needs me as badly as I want him. Sitting in his lap like this I can tease him just as effectively as he can tease me, so I rock my hips against him again, gyrating shamelessly.

"Olive." Brook's plaintive groan cuts straight through me as he nips at my neck. The need in his voice sends a shiver down my spine. I'm overcome with the desire to do something I've never found exciting before. I slither down his lap, running my hands down his chest as I go.

Kneeling in front of Brooks, I go for his belt buckle but he puts his hands on top to mine. "You don't have to do that, baby," he says through gritted teeth but I slap his hands away playfully.

"I want to. Give me what I want," I tell him as I work the zipper on his pants. Brooks growls and hauls me up, carrying me to the living room. I smack his chest ineffectively. "What are you doing? Put me down," I demand.

Brooks sets me down on my feet in front of the couch. "Carpet," he grunts. "Don't want you kneeling on the hard floor." A smirk slides across my lips as I slide back down to my knees. The plush white carpet is substantially more comfortable than the hard wood in the dining room. What a man, I think, as I slide my hands up his muscular thighs. He eyes me with dark hunger and shucks his pants and briefs in one go.

Brooks deftly unbuttons his shirt, letting it hang open. Sweet baby Jesus. He keeps doing things that I didn't even know were a turn on for me. The sight of his ridged abs peeking out of a dress shirt makes my mouth go dry and my pussy soaked. Yes, please.

He sits back on the couch, muscular arms thrown over the back and legs spread in a shameless display of masculinity. Not that he has an ounce of anything to be ashamed of. He knows it, judging by the cocky grin pulling up the corners of his sexy lips.

"Jesus, do you have to look so good naked?" I ask, arching a brow at him. "It's kind of unfair for the rest of us."

Brooks crooks a finger at me, stormy blue eyes locked on mine. "I'd rather look at you naked any day," he rumbles as I settle myself right between his legs. His cock looks achingly hard as it lays across his stomach. Now that I'm getting a good look at him I'm stunned he didn't break me in half when he fucked me last night. I don't know what deity he got on the good side of, but I need to figure it out and start making offerings.

Using just my fingertips, I trace a large vein up the side before gently circling the head. Brooks moans my name softly and drops his head to the back of the sofa as I wrap my hand around his hard length, giving him a slow stroke. A drop of moisture beads at the tip and I lean forward to lick it up, eliciting a shudder from Brooks.

I've only ever given head a couple of times and never enjoyed it before now. This makes me feel powerful and I want all of it. I'm dying to lick his turgid length, to take him deep in my mouth and taste him as I make him come down my throat. The more I imagine all the things I want to do to him, the wetter I get. I'm all in.

I swirl my tongue around the broad head of Brooks' dick before feeding the tip farther into my mouth. I can't take my eyes off his face. The tortured look of ecstasy is almost more than I can handle.

It's certainly enough encouragement to pull him deeper, working his cock with my hand and my mouth until he's trembling and I can feel him reaching the edge of his control. When he slides his hands through my hair, holding it away from my face in a gesture that's as much a caress as it is dominating, I moan around him.

"Oh fuck. Oh fuck, baby. God, yes! I'm going to come," he mutters, his breathing ragged. I hum happily and slow my pace, sucking harder, taking him deeper, deeper, until he's sliding past the back of my throat. Brooks explodes with an animalistic growl, cumming so hard I'm afraid I might have killed him. His whole body goes limp as I gingerly wipe my mouth.

"You alive, big guy?" I tease him, running my hands up and down his thigh. He doesn't move or respond at all except for the incoherent grunt that escapes his beautiful lips. Laughing, I lay my head on his bare thigh, stroking the hair covering his muscular calf. It's so soft I almost wonder if he conditions his leg hair and the thought makes me giggle.

Chapter 32: Brooks

I'm dead. She sucked the soul right out of my body through my dick. Holy hell, what a way to go. I'm vaguely aware of her soft cheek resting on my thigh and she's stroking my calf, giggling to herself.

"What's so funny down there? You better not be giggling at me after you just about killed me with that mouth of yours." Olive props her chin up on my leg to look at me, lips swollen, eyes bright and cheeks flushed. I pet her hair, smoothing it away from her face. "God, you're beautiful." My voice comes out gruffer than I intended, but I'm suddenly choked with emotion. I want to tell her I'm falling in love with her, but I don't want her to think I'm saying it just because she has the blowjob prowess of a porn star. So I keep my mouth shut and pull her up to cradle her in my lap. "I think I spend more time in your lap than out of it lately," she teases me.

"Good, it's where you belong," I tell her. She fits so perfectly snuggled into my chest like this. "You're wearing way too many clothes though." I slide my palm along her stomach, slowly seeking the tie of her dress, but she squeals and tries to jump out of my lap. "Where are you going, woman?" I demand.

She pushes off my chest, more forcefully this time, and I grudgingly let her stand. "I had a plan for this dress," she says coquettishly, lithe little fingers slowly pulling at the tie on her hip. My cock stirs in my lap again. She might literally kill me.

Olive unties the bow and slowly, provocatively, opens the sides of her dress, revealing her curvy body and the world's sexiest and most indecent black lingerie. Little gold details accentuate the edges, but everything else is sheer black mesh. Her rosy little nipples are peaked and I can see a faint glisten at the apex of her thighs. My mouth goes dry at the sight.

"Come here, Sugar." My words come out gravelly and, I think, pretty damn clear it's an order. Olive just grins and starts backing away slowly, heading away from the kitchen.

"Is your bedroom down this way?" She teases.

"It is, but that's beside the point," I growl. She takes another slow step backward, slipping her dress down her shoulders like a robe.

"Olive, I said come here," I'm still sitting on the couch but I sit up. "If I have to chase you I'm going to make you pay." It's more promise than threat.

She cocks an eyebrow at my lap where my dick has regained consciousness. In fact, his full attention is trained on Olive trying to sneak away in that sexy as fuck lingerie.

"You don't look like you'd mind catching me," she says primly, taking another step backwards. She lets the dress slide off one arm, holding it in one hand out to the side. She locks her eyes on mine before pointedly dropping it and taking another small step, daring me to follow.

Temptress. "Olive," I warn, coiling, ready to jump up and grab her. She spies the bunching of my muscles, and it gives her enough warning. She shrieks and giggles as she turns and runs towards my open bedroom door. The sight of her pert little ass running in those mesh panties has me on her, chasing her like a predator after a meal.

And I do intend to make a meal out of her.

I catch her just as she crosses the threshold, wrapping my arms around her middle in a bear hug before lifting her off the floor. Olive squeals and wriggles her curvy little body against my front. She's breathing hard, like she ran much more than 50 feet, and I like the feel of her ribcage expanding against my chest.

"You do realize it's more fun when you squirm like that?" I whisper in her ear. A shiver racks her body and her attempts to get loose morph into something more sensual. I growl and let her slip down my body until her feet rest on the floor, but I'm not ready to release her yet.

Firmly, I gather both of her tiny wrists behind her back and hold them in one hand. I pull her hair over one shoulder, giving me access to her neck and before wrapping my free arm across her chest, keeping her body close to mine. Pinned, and completely under my control. I pause, letting her breath a second, waiting to see if she tries to pull away but I'm deeply satisfied when she makes a purring moan and melts into my body.

"I told you I'd make you pay if you made me chase you, baby girl," I growl against her neck. Little goosebumps prick the skin of her chest as I slide a hand down to cup her tit.

My cock was already getting hard by the time I caught her and now it's at full attention, rubbing against her panty covered ass. It's all I can do to contain my groan when she arches back into my touch and wiggles her fingers, trying to wrap them around my dick.

Lifting her wrists to the side just out of reach, I make a tut tut noise. "Such a dirty girl. Is it my cock you want?"

Olive moans an inarticulate "mm-hm," as I knead her breast, teasing the nipple through the barely there material of her bra.

"Words, Sugar. I want to hear you say every dirty thing you're thinking."

"Yes," she gasps. "I like it. I want your cock."

I pinch her nipple, drawing another little gasp and moan out of her before responding. "Good girl. I'd give you what you want but I still have to punish you for running…" I make an exasperated sound, working my fingers over her opposite nipple and drawing out little moans.

Slipping my hand lower, I stroke her bare side and run my fingers along her ribs. "Maybe I should put you over my knee and spank you," I tease. Her breath hitches and she rubs her ass against me harder. "I think that turns you on. Is that what you want?"

Chapter 33: Olive

Oh Jesus. Is that what I want? Fuck yes. Which is crazy because I've never done anything like this before, but at this very moment, nothing could turn me on more. I'm finding lots of firsts with Brooks and each one has been better than the last.

I realize I've been thinking and not answering when Brooks grabs a handful of my ass and gives me a playful pat.

"Yes. Yes please," I answer breathily. Brooks sits on the edge of his bed. It's low and modern but looks comfortable, like most of his furniture. I don't have long to appreciate it though because a split second later, he has me bent over his lap like a disobedient child. My hands hit the floor.

I sputter because this wasn't exactly what I'd had in mind, but he quiets me with a smack to my butt cheek. It doesn't hurt, but the sound is surprising enough to stop my complaints. Brooks rubs the place he spanked, his touch seductive.

The way he has me positioned presses my sex into his muscular thigh and I'm finding a new appreciation for the male quadriceps.

"These panties are pure sin, Olive," he grumbles. "I can see how wet you are right through them." As if to make his point, his hard dick flexes and presses into my stomach. He slides his fingers down to slick over the wet mesh covering my pussy and it feels so fucking good that I can't help the moan working its way out of my throat.

Brooks palms my ass, rubbing in circles before lifting his hand to smack my other cheek. The sensation goes straight to my pussy, making my core clench as I shift against his thighs.

He keeps a sort of rhythm, spanking and rubbing until I'm wiggling with pleasure, my ass warm and tingling. Every nerve feels lit up with desire until I'm not sure if I want this to go on forever or if I just want him to fuck me now.

I quickly lose count, lost in the pattern and sensations when he pulls back his hand, making me think another smack is coming only to gently trail his fingers over my back, hips or thigh. The anticipation and tender caresses are the sweetest torture.

His questing fingers slip under the edge of my panties. I'm wet. So wet I'm almost embarrassed. Or I would be, except for the growl of appreciation that rumbles out of Brooks. The steel length of his dick presses into me, throbbing with his approval as he slides two fingers inside me.

"This is sexy as hell, dirty girl." He's practically vibrating with satisfaction, curling his fingers into my g-spot lazily until I'm dizzy with need. It's so insanely good, but I need more. Faster, harder, deeper.

"More," I whimper.

"More what? I told you I was going to make you so needy you'd beg for me to fuck you." His voice is low and heavy with lust.

"Arrogant ass," I sass back with a grin.

He has my back on the mattress so fast I don't even have time to register the shift before his massive body is on top of mine, limbs tangling with mine as he pins me down.

"God, I love it when you're mouthy," he groans. He grabs a condom from the nightstand and has it rolled on in record time. He slides inside of me in one long slow thrust, all the air in the room rushing out as we both gasp at the sensation of something so big being clasped so tight.

Brooks slips an arm under my shoulders, holding me close, and presses his forehead to mine as I hitch my legs around his hips.

"Fuck you feel good," He grunts as he thrusts into me. The angle of his rocking hips hits me just right and I'm already so wet. Fire curls in my belly, demanding release until I'm shaking and someone is pleading to come with each plunging stroke and I realize it's me.

Brooks pulls my hair to the side, exposing my neck, leaving soft warm kisses on my skin over and over again until the world shatters around me.

Chapter 34: Olive

I don't know how long we lay there in a haze, but the gentle stroking of fingertips over my ribs starts to tickle. I want to squirm away, but my body is limp and sated. I can put up with a little tickling. Until I can't. "Stop," I whine. "That tickles and you're about two seconds from getting kicked." Brooks chuckles but stops the tickling fingers. Rolling over onto my stomach so I can see his face better, I ask, "What are you doing on Christmas Eve?"

"Whatever you want me to do," Brooks replies with a cocky grin and an arched eyebrow.

"Be my date for Chelsea's wedding?" A couple hours ago I was terrified to ask him, afraid he wouldn't want to come with me. But now? Easy fucking peasy.

He gives me a sweet smile, his eyes doing that sexy crinkle thing that makes my heart speed up. "Yeah, I'd love that," he replies before pulling me on top of him and tucking the blanket around us. "On one condition." I peek up at him through my lashes, waiting for the cost. "You keep the DJ from playing any Bon Jovi songs."

I let out an evil cackle. "No promises. Sally lives for Bon Jovi."

"Are your bridesmaid friends going to be drinking and wooing again?"

"Sally and the Boston twins will absolutely be woo-girls. Me, not so much. But I am really looking forward to the reception. Plus I'm in charge of the cake so you know dessert is going to be on point."

"I've never been a fan of wedding cake but--"

I gasp, interrupting any "but" Brooks can come up with. "How can you not be a fan of wedding cake? That's sacrilege! Blasphemy!" I try to push off Brooks' chest but end up getting distracted by his big stupid muscles and let him pull me back down to kiss him with a disgruntled huff. I'm weak.

"As I was saying, I've never been a fan of wedding cake but I love everything you make so I'm excited to be there with you and eat your... cake."

"God, you're so dirty. I kind of love it."

"Oh you more than 'kind of' love it, baby girl." He peppers kisses down my jaw and neck, making me giggle. He's right. I really freaking love it. I'll take dirty talk over flowers and chocolate any day.

"What else can I expect at this wedding, besides the best wedding cake ever?"

"Open bar, music, dancing. All the good stuff. Oh. Um... this just occurred to me, but my family is going to be there. Like all of them."

Brooks just smiles bigger. "All of them? Even your Grandma?"

"Yup. Even Gran. And I guarantee you'll get to hear at least two good swears out of her."

"I can't wait." Brooks kisses me again before smacking my ass and making me yelp. "Oh god! Are you ok? Did I hurt you?" He panics and tries to look over my shoulder at my bare butt, but I'm laughing so hard that he can't get a good look.

"I'm fine," I get out between fits. "You just surprised me, that's all." He growls and holds me tighter.

"Do you have popcorn?" I ask. "I'd love some popcorn."

Brooks gives me a kiss and rolls me off him. "Of course, I have popcorn. Who doesn't have popcorn?"

"I don't know. Some people don't like popcorn. Satanists, probably."

Brooks laughs and shakes his head at me like I'm adorable as he heads to the closet and disappears. He returns a minute later wearing a pair of low slung gray jersey sleeper pants. I'm trying to contain my drooling when he tosses me a matching pair and a soft white t-shirt.

I bring them to my nose and sniff them shamelessly because I love the way they smell like him. He leans down and kisses me silly before snatching two pillows and the blanket from his bed.

"Get dressed. I'm going to make you some popcorn."

"Can I snoop through your bathroom?" I call out as I watch his sexy as hell butt walk away.

"Knock yourself out, Sugar," he calls back as he leaves the bedroom.

Grinning to myself, I jump up and put on the clothes. I have to roll up the bottoms and tighten the drawstring up a ridiculous amount but I love it. I've never been so comfy.

Brooks' bathroom is insane. I may never go home again after seeing his tub. If I had to guess, I'd say it is big enough to hold three full-grown adults. And then there is the massive walk-in shower with two overhead shower heads. Yup. I am never going to make Brooks shower at my apartment again.

By the time I've cleaned myself up and poked through Brooks' toiletries, smelling everything, I can hear the microwave beeping and the scent of buttery popcorn is wafting through the open door.

Following my nose, I find Brooks on the couch with his blanket, hot popcorn waiting for me on the coffee table. He lifts up one side of the blanket for me to snuggle in next to him.

Chapter 35: Brooks

The next few days pass by in a blur. Olive stays at my house every night, letting me drive her home after work and back every morning. I thought it would be a struggle to convince her, but she said that my shower was reason enough. I love spending every evening with her, even if we just sit side by side working on our laptops until I take her to bed.

On Christmas Eve, we sleep in late. Olive finished Chelsea's wedding cake last night and the bakery is closed until the day after Christmas. I shut down all construction so my employees can all have the next few days off to spend time with their families.

For the first time since Olive and I got together, there is nothing for us to worry about and we can lie around in bed all morning. I take advantage of the extra time by making love to Olive slowly and making her come over and over until she's a boneless, happy mess.

We shower together before I take her back to the bakery. She has to deliver the cake, which she insisted on doing with Lilah since they have a weird sister mind link thing when it comes to moving cakes. Then she's meeting up with Chelsea, and the other bridesmaids to get ready. I won't get to see her until the wedding this evening and the thought makes me scowl.

It's the most time we've spent apart in more than a week and it makes me feel antsy. I just want to be near her but I know I'm being possessive so I try to shove those thoughts down as I drop her off.

She waves to me from the door and starts to go inside but I roll down my window and call out, "No strippers!"

She gives me a thumbs up and an eye-roll before ducking inside.

My drive back home is lonely. Walking back into my house, it feels too big and quiet. I've gotten used to Olive being here with me, flopped on the sofa in her fluffy socks while she does her payroll or places orders.

Was I really worried she wouldn't like my house? I've practically got her moved in at this point. Smiling to myself, I pick up the throw blanket she tossed over the back of our couch and fold it neatly before laying it back where she likes it. All of her hair and makeup stuff has made its way over in the last week. She even hung a razor in my shower. A single trip with one of my cargo vans would probably be enough to get everything else.

Would it be a dick move to pack her stuff up and move her in while she's getting ready for the wedding? Definitely a dick move, I say to myself. I'll get her moved in soon enough but if I don't at least ask her first, she'd probably lose her shit and then I'd have Lilah and Luis over here making good on their threats.

Grabbing my duffle bag from the closet, I pack everything I need to stay at the hotel with Olive tonight. I'm careful to stash her Christmas present down in the corner under my socks so she doesn't see it.

Chapter 36: Olive

I'm in a lovesick haze by the time Brooks drops me off at the bakery. It almost feels weird to be back in my apartment, especially alone. I haven't been alone in days. I always thought that would bother me. That being in a relationship would mean giving up my alone time.

I usually like my time alone. I like to sit by myself when I do my paperwork or read, but more and more I'm realizing that I'd rather sit with Brooks.

I quickly double check my overnight bag to make sure I haven't forgotten anything, toss it in my car and wait for Lilah to arrive. She's coming to help me load up Chelsea and Matt's cake. We've been working on the sugar flowers and intricate decorations for two weeks. It's six tiers of perfection and sugary heaven… and now that it's stacked on its double-strength wood base and boxed up, it's too heavy for me to move on my own.

Brooks offered to help, but Lilah is my ride-or-die cake delivery girl. We've done enough of these that we move in tandem without even thinking about it. Plus, I'd strangle Brooks if he dropped it. I'm not allowed to strangle my sister.

I spot Lilah pulling into the parking lot, five minutes early because she's amazing, and I grab the envelope with the place cards with all the flavors for each tier. The kitchen at the hotel will cut everything and put the plates back out, but I don't want guests to be confused about the flavors.

Chelsea gave me free rein with the cake flavors, so I made all of my favorite things. Gingerbread cake with spiced mousse, vanilla bean cake with winter citrus curd, lemon poppyseed with raspberry preserves, devil's food with dark chocolate hazelnut mousse, coconut cake tres leches with passionfruit curd. The top tier is Chelsea's favorite cake and the flavor I make her every year for her birthday: confetti cake with vanilla buttercream. Admittedly, not the fanciest combination, but I know how happy it will make her.

Lilah bounces into the kitchen, fresh faced and cheerful. "I found a house! I'm putting in an offer on Monday!" she announces proudly.

"You did?! Where?" She's been looking for her own place for weeks; apartment living and roommates have finally lost their appeal.

Lilah's grin gets even bigger. "That's the best part! It's only a 10 minute drive from you!"

My brain short circuits for a second and I excitedly ask, "You're buying in Napa?"

My sister gives me a look like I've lost my mind. "Napa? Why would I buy in Napa? No... it's on the outskirts of Sonoma..."

"Oh, duh! Ten minutes from here. From the bakery and my apartment," I try to recover. It doesn't work. Lilah eyes me like I've lost my mind.

"I know you've been spending a lot of time with Brooks in Napa but you didn't move in with him while I wasn't paying attention, did you?"

"No! I swear, I just had a brain fart. I need coffee. You want some coffee?"

Lilah just looks at me suspiciously.

"Never mind. Let's get coffee at the hotel. I want to get the cake delivered safely first."

***

Lilah and I load the cake into the delivery van with practiced ease. Our bags and dresses carefully arranged, we make the quick drive to the hotel. The cake is safely stored in the kitchen fridge, though the chef grumbles that he had to reorganize his walk-in to make room for such a large cake. What did he expect with 300 guests? What a grump.

With the cake safely tucked away, Lilah leaves to get ready with Gran and Julia, while I head up to the hotel bridal suite to get ready with Chelsea and the bridesmaids.

Chelsea spoils the living hell out of us.

I'm pretty sure Matt set everything up because that's just the kind of guy he is. Chelsea doesn't come from money like he does and it seems like he goes out of his way to make sure she gets the best of everything, especially when it came to their wedding day. If he had better taste in groomsmen, this day would be just about perfect. I shudder thinking about the groomsmen I got paired up with. I'm taking one for the team, but the guy gives me the creeps.

We're buffed, polished, and moisturized from head to toe in the hotel spa before meeting the hair stylists and makeup artists back in the hotel suite. Room service surprised us with an alarming number of chocolate-covered strawberries and several bottles of Chelsea's favorite Prosecco. Thank god Chelsea was still having her hair done and hadn't gotten to makeup because she started sobbing when she read the card they brought from Matt.

It takes a small army of beauty professionals to get us ready, but they are cheerfully efficient. I finally get a quiet moment alone with Chelsea to thank her for letting me bring Brooks at the last minute.

"Oh, I added him to the guest list the night I bailed on dinner with you," she smirks knowingly.

"It feels weird to say but I think I owe you a thank you for ditching me. That was quite the sneaky operation you and Lilah pulled off."

Chelsea lets out a pleased laugh. "Yeah, it's a good thing I only talked to you through text messages though. I'm not sure I could have pulled it off if we spoke on the phone. I almost felt bad about it when I saw you guys leave the bar together but... well... It seemed to work out fine."

She blushes and changes the subject. "I'm happy you two finally figured things out. Just keep Brooks away from Matt tonight. It turns out, Matt figured out the stripper thing Sally had planned, found the poor guy and paid him a lot of money to not show up. He wasn't pleased that some random guy showed up and took his shirt off, anyway."

I laugh at the look on Chelsea's face. "He almost took off his pants too. Remember he--"

Chelsea holds up a hand to interrupt me. "Nope. He just took off his shirt. And if you want your boyfriend to stay alive, that should probably be all anyone remembers from the bachelorette party."

I clink my champagne flute against hers gently. "I'm down with that. I'd rather no one except me saw him in his underwear ever again."

Chelsea gives me a wink and a one-armed hug. "I'm so happy for you. I know it's not easy for you to let people in, but you're one of my best friends and I just want you to be as happy as I am."

My lip feels a little wobbly as I hug her back. "Thank you, Chelsea. I'm happy for you too."

"Good!" Chelsea wipes away a rogue tear before straightening her spine. "No more sappy stuff. Get ready and let's go party."

It takes forever but finally my long hair is curled, pinned, tucked, and sprayed into a style that I couldn't hope to recreate in my lifetime. My stylist tucks a floral hairpiece with eucalyptus and roses into the design before declaring me done.

The makeup artists give all the bridesmaids soft smokey eyes and way too much foundation, blush, and bronzer to be healthy. The false eyelashes they put on us look amazing, but they are already starting to bug the hell out of me. Luckily, I manage to talk my makeup artist down on the contouring. She was coming at me with a contour stick like a woman on a mission and I was afraid Brooks was going to have a hard time recognizing me if she got her way.

We finally get to put on our dresses and help Chelsea into her wedding dress. She found a Maggie Sottero ivory silk gown with a sheer overlay covered in Art Deco style crystal beading. It's 1920s princess in the front, but the open back screams sex appeal.

It's perfect. It makes me wonder if Brooks and I will have a wedding like this. What would it be like to walk down the aisle and see him waiting for me?

The champagne is clearly going to my head. Shaking off the yearning thoughts, I slip into my bridesmaid dress. Thank god Chelsea has amazing taste. A less thoughtful bride might have frumped up her bridesmaids but Chelsea is nothing if not kind to her friends. She had Sally order each of us a forest green silk gown that is nothing short of sexy. The plunging neckline takes a little creative arranging but oh my god, is it worth it.

When it's finally time to go downstairs, we collect our bouquets and follow Chelsea. We keep having to remind her to slow down because she's so excited to get downstairs to Matt. It's equal parts sweet and annoying because we are all terrified she's going to trip on her dress and end up face first on the hotel floor. Sally and I end up hooking elbows on each side of her to keep her safe.

I can't blame her for being so antsy. I'm dying to get back to Brooks and it's not even my wedding. I've become so used to being near him all day. Now it sucks to be apart for so long.

The ballroom is set up for one hell of a party. Matt and Chelsea opted to have a quick ceremony at the beginning and just jump straight into the reception. Guests are already seated at their tables by the time we get downstairs.

We line up right outside the door, shepherded around by the wedding planner/ border collie in human form. One by one we walk up the aisle to the music, smiling at guests while focusing on the most important tasks: never lock your knees, and don't faceplant in the aisle.

The ballroom is lit up with thousands of white Christmas lights. Fir trees are spread along the walls, decorated with more white lights and white and silver ornaments. The four bars are prepared with festive cocktails and there's even a hot chocolate bar with every topping and stir in we could come up with. (Marshmallows made by yours truly.)

Brooks catches my eye as soon as I walk into the room, grinning at me from a table near the front. I smile back, and make sure my next step is long enough to show him the way the dress is slit up my left thigh. I think I can hear him audibly groan from 20 feet away and I smile even harder.

The flower girl, Matt's little cousin, takes one look at the crowd, throws her basket of fake flower petals in the air and bolts for her mommy. Chelsea and Matt spend the entire ceremony smiling so hard that I'm afraid one of them is going to get a cheek cramp.

I try hard to focus on the ceremony, but the sight of Brooks seated just a little way away is too hard to resist. Even when I look away, I can feel him watching me. I can feel how much he wants me, feel the places he put his mouth all over my body this morning.

We finally make it through the ceremony and the wedding party walks back down the aisle to go take pictures. What I really want to do is run and jump into Brooks' lap. Not that he would mind, but the wedding planner might stab me with a faux icicle if I don't show enough decorum. So I blow him a kiss as we head back out to take pictures.

Luckily, Chelsea puts her foot down after 15 minutes and demands that we all go back in and enjoy hors d'oeuvres and cocktails. Bride of the year over here.

Chapter 37: Brooks

The sight of Olive walking down the aisle, flashing her very long and very bare leg was truly one of the sexiest things I've ever seen. A lesser man would have jumped up and held the pieces of her skirt together so no one could see what's mine.

Not that holding the skirt in place would do any good. Between the low-cut neckline, exposed back, and the way the fabric slips over her body, Olive looks like walking sin. And, with nary a panty line in sight, I spent more time eying my girl and speculating whether she has panties on than I should admit.

Her little wink nearly did me in as she swung her cute ass out of the ballroom with the rest of the wedding party but I held it together, picking up a beer and a Christmas-themed cocktail from one of the bars, and waiting by a tall cocktail table for Olive to come back.

We wait for what feels like forever but finally the wedding party is announced and the soft classical music that has been playing gives way to "The Best Day of My Life" and the bridesmaids and groomsmen come dancing back into the ballroom in pairs followed by the bride and groom. They take the dance floor, tearing it up while the music blasts.

I'm good right up until I see the groomsmen that came dancing into the room with Olive take her hand, spin her out and back in, and then leer at her cleavage. What really took the cake, though, is the tight look on her face. He's a scumbag, and he's making my woman uncomfortable.

I've been patient all day, but the elastic band that's been holding me back snaps. He's got his hands and his eyes on what's mine. Hell. Fucking. No.

I cross the room, weaving through the tables and doing my best not to stomp. The groomsman clearly sees me coming and the look on my face must be enough of a warning because the lecherous look falls off his and he lets Olive go like she's made of lava. I take Olive's hand and pull her close, careful of the crazy ass heels she's wearing, dip her low and kiss the hell out of her.

I'm not trying to make a scene. Or maybe I am. I really don't give a fuck. I'm going to lay claim to this woman, and make sure no one else touches her ever again. Maybe I should feel guilty about being such a caveman but the way Olive melts into me, throwing her arms around my neck and kissing me back with just as much fervor, makes any guilt I might have vanish. She seems perfectly happy for me to publicly mark my territory.

I'm so wrapped up in the satisfaction of holding her, the silky soft skin of her exposed back against my hand, and the little hums of pleasure Olive is making that it takes me a long time to realize people are applauding and hooting all around us. The bride and bridesmaids are cat calling with Sally, cheering, "Get it!"

Olive blushes but smiles at me like I'm the greatest thing she's ever seen as I pull her up. She fans her face, smiling at her friends. "I think I need a drink!" Taking her hand, I lead her back to the table and her waiting drink. Eyes follow us for a minute, but soon the room is focused on the bride and groom again.

"You got this for me?" she asks, picking up the cocktail.

"Yeah, the bartender called it a mistletoe cocktail, which I thought was a terrible name because mistletoe is actually poisonous. He said it's just gin, cranberry juice, and elderflower liqueur."

Olive grins at me as I ramble, her soft smile hiding a thought that I can't read.

"What?" I ask.

She runs a hand up my arm, smoothing my tie and trailing her soft little palm down my chest. "You're just so much... more than I expected when I met you."

I'm speechless, my heart skipping and then tripping over itself to catch up.

"I don't know what I did in a past life to deserve you, Olive." Brushing the back of my knuckles over her soft cheek I start to say more but we're pulled out of the moment by the collective "Ooh!" of the wedding guests as the staff bring a truly enormous cake out of the kitchen.

It takes two full-grown men to carry it and they still look like they're struggling. They almost make it to the cake table before one of them catches a toe on a taped down power cord and stumbles. The entire crowd gasps and sucks in a breath, holding it as the poor guy regains his footing and they both manage to keep the cake upright. A lone pinecone topples off one of the tiers, but otherwise the cake makes it to the table unharmed.

There is a loud whoosh of people exhaling in relief. The server looks pale as a sheet and is visibly trembling as he makes a bee line back to the kitchen. Olive is gripping my bicep so tightly I'm worried she's going to break a finger. I'm going to have little fingernail bruises there tomorrow.

She lets out a relieved laugh as she releases my arm, shaking out her fingers. Chelsea meets her eyes across the room and gives her the finger guns and a wink, making Olive giggle. She shoots her friend the 'OK' sign before turning around and downing the rest of her drink.

"I think my soul almost left my body there for a second," she says.

Chapter 38: Olive

For a second, when the waiter tripped with Chelsea's cake, I wondered how hard it would be to hide a body. Now, however, with the cake safely on the table, I'm feeling more charitable towards the poor guy. I bet he was wondering how fast he would lose his job at the same moment I was contemplating my legal defense.

Shaking myself and releasing my death grip on Brooks' arm, I relax just a bit. God, that was terrifying.

Brooks slips a warm hand down my back, his work-roughened hand caressing the exposed skin as he leads me towards the cake table. Lilah is headed in our direction and I can see the rest of my family sitting a couple tables back.

There's a small crowd admiring the cake as Lilah meets up with us, grinning maniacally. "How close was that?" she asks.

"Oof," I reply. "Way too close for that waiter's safety," I grin back. She scoops the fallen pinecone off the floor and sighs. I know what she's thinking. What a waste of chocolate. We hand-crafted each one, filling them with soft caramel and spiced ganache.

"Brooks," Lilah nods in his direction.

"Lilah," he replies with a salute.

She laughs and leans in. "Gran sent me over to drag you guys back to our table. She wants the dirt on you two since you haven't brought this guy to family dinner yet. She says she's running out of patience."

"Alright, alright. We'll go over in a second. I just want Brooks to see the finished cake before another disaster can befall it." Looking out to my Gran, I hold up a finger and silently ask her to give me a minute before pulling Brooks closer to the cake.

He holds me close as I point out the finer details. The gum paste flowers, crystalized berries, the chocolate curls that look like cinnamon sticks and the chocolate pinecones, airbrushed and painstakingly hand-painted to look real.

"I get wedding cakes now," he speaks low so only I can hear him. His nose gently brushing my neck. His palm slides around to my stomach, pulling my back flush with his front.

Now would be a very inconvenient time to get turned on. I'm supposed to drag Brooks over to meet my family in a minute and I really can't do that with soaking wet panties. Oh, wait! I'm not wearing any because this stupid beautiful dress will show panty lines if I even think about undergarments. Christ. I'm going to have to excuse myself to clean up if he doesn't stop it.

With a sigh, I remove Brooks' hand and lead him towards my family. Might as well get this over with. Pulling up to the table, I kiss Gran on the cheek before introducing her to Brooks.

"Brooks, this is--"

"So nice to finally meet you, Brooks. Call me Gran!" she interrupts. "Don't roll your eyes at me, Olive," she chastises while shaking Brooks' hand and simultaneously feeling up his bicep.

"Hands off the goods, Gran," I tell her as I peel her hands off my man. "She's handsy," I faux whisper to Brooks. He's grinning broadly and winks at Gran. She melts so hard I'm surprised she doesn't bust a hip and hit the ground.

"Everyone else, this is Brooks." I gesture at my siblings as I give him their names. "Asher, Lukas, and Julia."

Asher and Lukas both stand up to shake his hand. Julia waves from her chair. My brothers immediately start in on the build outs they want to do at the shop, asking Brooks a million questions. Julia stands, excusing herself to use the bathroom. I've had to pee for ages so I try to sneak off with her, patting Brooks' arm as I go. I don't make it more than a step before he pulls me back for a kiss.

"Don't disappear on me for too long. I just got you back after waiting all day," he whispers in my ear. It pleases me more than I should admit that he missed me today. I was so busy, but I missed him too. He was on my mind all day. All I really wanted to do was to hurry things along and get back by his side.

I swear I can feel his eyes watching me all the way out of the ballroom. Sure enough, turning to look back at him as we get to the heavy double doors, he's still talking to my brothers but his eyes are glued on me. He's positively smoldering, and it sends pleasure skittering up my spine.

Julia and I wait in line and then giggle while we both awkwardly wrangle our gowns in stalls next to each other. A floor length silk gown sounds great in theory and looks amazing for photos and dancing but no one stops to think about the logistics of trying to hold it up out of the way without wrinkling the shit out of it while you pee.

We wash our hands next to each other and take a second to touch up our makeup. Julia adjusts her boobs and straightens the top of her burgundy velvet gown. It's off the shoulder and clings to her curves like a second skin.

"Brooks is quite the catch, huh?" she asks me nonchalantly as she carefully wipes a fleck of mascara from under her eye. The question comes out way too innocent.

Sighing, I put down my lip gloss. "Just say what you're thinking. I know there was a ton of subtext hidden in that comment and I'm too tired to pull the truth out of you by force."

Julia grins, pausing with her lipstick hovering over her lips. "I mean, we haven't gotten to talk much the last few weeks." She holds a hand up before I can apologize. "Not your fault. I've been working at the hospital and studying 24/7. It's just… I don't know what I expected when you told me you were dating your contractor. I guess I just didn't realize he was such a daddy."

Lilah walks in at that very moment and stops dead, "Brooks is a dad?"

Julia smiles at our shocked faces. "No, not like that. At least I'm assuming not. I mean, he's a *daddy*. You know, a little older, salt and pepper on the sides, super big and muscly, those little smile lines around his eyes, likes to get all caveman when someone touches his woman… If the internet has taught me one thing, that man is a daddy."

Oh, dude. "Julia, I swear to god, if you call him a daddy one more time, I will end you."

"Relax, I'm not about to encourage the rumors of the Donovan's collective daddy issues. That's just like the internet definition of him. Besides, I'm not here to yuck your yum. I've got my own fish to fry." She applies her lipstick and wiggles her eyebrows at her reflection in the mirror.

"Oh yeah? Have you been 'frying a bunch of fish' at school?" Lilah asks with her finger quotes.

"Oh tons," Julia answers sarcastically. "I go to school with a shit ton of women and male nurses. Not a dominating Latin Lover among them." She sighs resentfully, her green eyes sharp as she wipes her finger gingerly at the edge of her red lipstick.

"Are you still waiting for Javier to come back?" I ask her gently. "Luis says he hates New York. Maybe he'll move back home. Tons of wineries need marketing."

For a second, Julia looks so lost and sad, every bit the innocent little kid we grew up protecting, but she quickly straightens her spine and smooths her retro-curled hair. "He's not coming back and I'm not waiting for him." Her voice is firm, and it sounds like a mantra she's been repeating. "I just won't settle for less than something... big."

Rubbing a hand over her back, I try to soothe the unhappiness out of her. "Good," I tell her. "You shouldn't settle for less than that."

Julia sheds the vulnerability like a lizard shedding a skin, visibly shaking it off before heading towards the door. "Let's get drunk and dance. With any luck, we can get your man to have another alpha moment." She winks at me, holding the door open for us with a sweep of her arm.

***

As it turns out, the rest of the night is basically one big, never-ending "alpha moment" with Brooks. He stays by my side the entire night and practically growls if another man comes too close to me.

If it were anyone else, it would be annoying, but with Brooks... I'm good. It makes me feel all warm and fuzzy and, if I'm being honest, super turned on. He holds me close while we dance, pulls me into his lap when we sit, and insists I change into my comfortable flats when my feet start to hurt. I didn't even say anything, he just knew.

As I'm changing my shoes, sitting in Brooks' lap, Julia wanders by, gives me a conspiratorial wink, and stage-whispers "Daddy," with an 'I told you so' look on her face.

"Fuck off," I whisper back, swatting her butt with my flat and leaving a satisfying dust print on her velvet dress before slipping the shoe on my foot. She brushes the mark away with exaggerated indignation.

"Did your sister just call me daddy?" Brooks looks alarmed and a little pale.

"Oh my god," I laugh, putting my head in my hands. I try not to die laughing. "Just ignore her."

"What's so funny?" he asks, pulling me closer.

"She's just being a brat. Trust me, you're not her type."

"As long as I'm your type, that's all that matters."

Cupping his face with both hands, I kiss him and stroke his beard. "You are very much my type. In fact, 'my type' is very specific, and it includes only you."

He gives me a long, soft kiss; it goes on so long I forget to breathe and start to feel a little dizzy. Or maybe he just makes me feel like that.

Once the catering staff brings the pieces of cake back out, Brooks deposits me in my own chair and goes to get us each a piece. He comes back balancing six little dessert plates on his ridiculously muscled forearms. Someone must have helped load him up.

"What are you doing?" I laugh as he rejoins me, balancing the little plates carefully.

"Being greedy," he replies while I help him set them all on the table in front of us. "My woman made the cake and I'm proud of her," he says with a wink. "Besides, how am I supposed to make an educated decision about wedding cake without tasting all of them?"

He gleefully feeds me a bite of the gingerbread cake before taking a bite himself. I can't help the triumphant smirk that spreads across my face as I watch him taste each flavor, rolling his eyes in ecstasy. Wedding cake is obviously amazing.

Chelsea calls all the single ladies to the dance floor for the bouquet toss, but I sit contentedly in Brooks' lap, watching as Julia drags Lilah out with her. Chelsea has deadly aim as she launches it behind her. It sails straight at Lilah's head, but she screams and ducks, letting Julia snatch it out of the air.

Brooks and I drink and dance the rest of the night away, his broad body enveloping me as we move together. The party seems to move around us but I feel consumed by Brooks, too wrapped up in the way he feels pressed against me to care that there are other people in the room. I'm dying to get out of here and back up to my hotel room.

Chapter 39: Brooks

Torture. Sweet fucking torture. That's how I spend my Christmas Eve. With Olive barely concealed in green silk like a sexy present just waiting to be unwrapped. Every swing of her hips and shimmy of her body as she dances winds me up more and more.

If this was any other event, I would have hauled her sweet ass out of here and been balls deep inside of her warm pussy hours ago. But she's a bridesmaid, and her friend is important to her. So I spend hour after hour trying to ignore the climbing desperation to get her body underneath mine.

I thought I was doing a pretty good job right up until the bride and groom made their exit under a tunnel of sparklers, held aloft by the bridal party. The sight of Olive grinning broadly, laughing under the dancing lights makes my breath hitch. She catches me watching her as the crowd starts to disperse and gives me a sly grin, sliding the slit of her dress just a little higher.

Using one finger I beckon her towards me, making sure she can see from the look on my face that it's a command, not a request. My control is stretched so thin I'm afraid it will snap and I'll just fuck her right here in front of everyone. She makes her way towards me, slowly, clearly aware of the effect she's having.

When she gets close enough, I put a possessive hand on the back of her neck and pull her close. Her breasts press against my chest and I can feel the silk of her dress slip between us as she bites her lip and looks at me, eyes burning and hooded with lust.

Making sure no one is close enough to hear what I'm about to say, I lean down to whisper in her ear.

"You've been teasing me all night with that dress. No bra. No panties. Just that silk sliding over your curves, torturing me."

Olive grins at me, eyes lit with mischief. "If I've been such a bad girl maybe you need to punish me?"

Fuck me.

"Room, now," I snap and it makes Olive giggle.

Olive takes great delight in rubbing against me like a cat on the elevator ride up to our room, knowing full well I can't do anything about it while there are so many people packed in with us. As soon as we exit and the doors shut behind us I throw her over my shoulder and stomp to our room. She squeals and laughs as she smacks my butt, demanding to be put down. She should know by now that won't work.

Tossing her on the bed, I rip my tie from my neck and throw it across the room. She watches me hungrily as I unbutton my shirt, biting her lower lip as I remove the cuff links and set them on the desk.

She draws one leg up, letting it rise out of the slit of her dress. She's a goddamn temptress, like a ripe piece of fruit in front of a starving man. "If you like that dress you better take it off before I get my hands on it," I growl in warning.

Olive gets to her knees on the bed and unzips the side of the dress before slowly sliding it over her head. It doesn't matter how many times I've seen her naked. I'll never get enough. She's all smooth skin with dusky pink nipples, peaked with arousal, begging to be sucked. And her adorable little belly button. Why the fuck is it so cute?

Pushing her back down on the mattress, I place her hands on the headboard. "Don't move your hands. If you do, I'll stop. Do you hear me?"

She nods with rapt attention, dark tendrils of hair falling out of her carefully styled braids. Grabbing her thighs, I spread her open for me, and watch her eyes roll back in her head as I give her a long slow lick. I keep tonguing her at a languid pace as she moans. Like I have all the time in the world. And really, I do. Because I'm going to make Olive mine and eat this pussy every night for as long as I live.

Olive tries to arch into me, squirming against my patient mouth, but I hold her down with firm hands on her thighs.

"Oh, no you don't." I rumble at her. "You be still while I dole out your punishment."

She lets out a pleased little sigh. "This doesn't seem like much of a punishment."

Chuckling, I bite down on her inner thigh just enough to leave a mark and make a gasp slip from her lips.

"I'm going to lick this pussy once for every filthy thought that dress put in my head."

I give her other thigh a little matching bite. "Then I'm going to lick it once for each time I caught another man looking at you in it."

"That's not fair," she complains. "That's like victim blaming-- Oh!" She interrupts herself as I slide a finger inside her.

"Oh fuck. You're so wet. Did you get yourself all worked up teasing me? Wiggling in my lap. Grinding your ass into my cock while you danced. This little pussy wants me bad, doesn't it?" Slipping my finger in and out of her makes obscenely wet sucking sounds. Sounds that go straight to my dick, already painfully hard and aching to be released.

Wait your turn, I remind it. Olive loves this game. Her pliant body giving away just how much as she moans, her pussy tightening around my finger, trying to find enough friction to make her see Jesus.

She moans as I pull my finger from her tightness, sucking her juices off of it. "Don't worry, Sugar. I'm going to take care of you. I'll always take care of you. You just have to be patient."

Chapter 40: Olive

I hate being patient.

Brooks holds my thighs apart, watching me with his piercing blue eyes as he tortures me, slowly licking my folds. Each gentle graze of his tongue over my clit sends jolts of pleasure spiraling through my core.

I don't know how long he keeps me on the edge. It feels like hours and I'm desperate to come, needing just a little more, but he won't give it to me. I'm a whimpering wet mess as he holds me in place, pinning my hips to the mattress until I start begging.

"Please, please, please, Brooks, please!" I cry out, throwing my head back.

"You keep those beautiful eyes on me and tell me whose pussy this is when you come," he growls, his beard rubbing my thigh.

Nodding frantically, I lock eyes with him as he pulls my clit between his lips, pulling and suckling as his fingers work inside me. The tight ache and desperation gives way as my world swirls with pleasure and overwhelming relief.

Brooks doesn't stop when I come. He barely even slows down before demanding, "More."

God help me, I don't think I could stop coming if I tried. Not with his mouth on my clit, warm and insistent and his fingers working inside me like they're made of pure magic. One peak rolls into another until I've lost count and nearly screamed myself hoarse.

Brooks finally lets up, but there's a fire burning in his eyes as he flips me over onto my stomach. I hear him unbuckle his belt. His pants hit the floor and I look back, watching hungrily as he dons a condom. He gives my ass a quick smack before yanking my hips back up to meet his.

I'm still so sensitive that I cry out as he rubs the length of his cock against my pussy, slipping it between my folds. He's using me to lube himself up, and it's so fucking dirty. I. Love. It.

Using his knee, Brooks pushes my legs farther apart, spreading me wide with a growl of satisfaction. He wraps my hair around his fist with one hand, using the other to press the fat head of his cock against my slit, letting me feel just how big he is. The pulsing in my clit becomes a thumping, fervent drumbeat. A reminder that Brooks is the only man who can make me feel this way.

"Are you going to take all of me in that tight little pussy?" he asks with a groan, slipping just an inch inside of me before pulling back out.

"Oh my god," I moan. "Yes, all of it! I want it, please!"

He thrusts into me so deep and so hard my world spins. Brooks' unending control seems to snap as he grips my hips with bruising force and pistons into me, shaking and gritting his teeth as he tells me every filthy thing he's thinking.

"Jesus Christ, that's fucking sexy. Look at that ass bounce while I fuck you. God, I love that tight little pussy. Nothing in the world feels as good as your sweet little cunt wrapped around my dick. Taking every fucking inch. God damn, baby."

I don't know if he even realizes he's saying everything out loud. I lose myself in the rhythm and the pleasure coursing through me. So lost that I'm on the verge of coming again without realizing until my thighs start to tremble and my stomach tightens

"Ah! God, that's it," Brooks moans. "Come on my dick. Get it all slippery for me so I can fuck you harder." He pulls my hair back making my spine arch and I come on a breathless scream.

"Fuck, that's so good." His pace becomes frantic and chaotic as he teeters on the edge. The clenching of my sex as I come is too much for Brooks' control. "Fuck-fuck-fu--" Brooks comes deep inside me with a roaring groan before collapsing sideways on the bed, pulling me into him.

I don't even remember falling asleep but I must have because the next thing I know, I wake up to the feeling of someone moving me. Brooks lays me carefully on the pillow before pulling the blanket up over us and tucking me in.

***

I wake up on Christmas morning with the barest hint of a hangover, a painfully dry mouth, and the complete certainty that I've got a raging case of smudged mascara.

The other half of the king-size bed is empty but I can hear the shower running and Brooks singing a charmingly off-key version of "White Christmas." The man is as adorable as he is potent.

Sitting up and yawning, I pat my hair and let out a small, "Oh no." Leaning over just a little, I can see my reflection in the mirror hanging over the desk and… yikes.

My hair mostly escaped its bobby pin hell from last night. That would be bad enough but the lethal combination of all the hair product the stylist used, Brooks' roaming hands, and a hard night's sleep have left me with a crazy nest of hair that is somehow both sticking out and horribly flat. It is a decidedly bad look for me.

The water shuts off in the bathroom and I frantically look for a way to clean myself up. It's only been a couple weeks since I started seeing Brooks and it's still way too soon to drop this kind of scary on him.

Shockingly, there's no magic spray within arms reach that will cure my sad panda face, rat's nest hair, and offensive morning breath. What kind of world do we live in? Why has no one made this yet?!

The bathroom door creaks a little as it opens and I panic, throwing the sheet over my head without planning an exit strategy. Cool. This is my life now. I'll just lay here under a sheet like a stinky ghost until I can convince Brooks to look the other way while I slink off to the bathroom.

I hear his chuckle, so warm and smooth he sounds like good chocolate. "What are you doing under there?" His weight settles on the bed next to me and he tries to tug the sheet down but I keep a good grip on it.

"Don't look at me!"

"Don't be ridiculous, Olive. I already saw you when I got up and you look beautiful." He tries to pull the sheet down again.

Huffing, I hold firm. "Clearly you were looking at someone else."

He laughs again and I can hear him rummaging around for a couple of seconds before I feel a hand sneaking under the sheet. I'm about to abandon my grip on the top of the sheet so I can defend myself from his wandering magical hands but the arm moves unexpectedly and instead of tickling me or trying to steal my cover it holds his phone in front of my face.

On the screen is a selfie of a groggy, shirtless Brooks with sexy-as-fuck rumpled hair. His free arm is holding the phone but his other arm is cradling me to his chest, crazy hair, smudged mascara and all.

And oh god. The way he's looking at me. It makes my heart thump out of rhythm and pound in my ears. I can see so clearly how much he loves me.

I've been loved by my mother and siblings. My grandmother loves me. But no man has ever looked at me like that. Like I'm his entire world, his gravity, and his reason for breathing.

I've seen little glimpses of that look for weeks. It was there when he shook my hand and refused to let it go, when he found me at the bar and stole my purse. It was there every time he touched me.

"You win," I tell him quietly. "I'm coming out but don't laugh at me."

"Never," he rumbles as I peek over the sheet. He's wrapped a towel around his waist but he's still wet from the shower and there are droplets of water running down his chest. God, I want to trace those with my tongue.

"Don't look at me like that if you want to shower before breakfast," he warns me, a dark smile lifting one side of his mouth. Oh lord, he's so tempting, but I catch a whiff of my morning breath and sigh.

"Sorry, I definitely need a shower," I tell him as I throw back the sheet and scoot my bare ass to the bathroom, making sure I give him a little extra sway as I go. He makes a gratifying groan and flops back on the bed.

The hotel shower isn't as good as the one at Brooks' house, but it still beats the hell out of my apartment shower. Fifteen minutes of scrubbing, exfoliating, conditioning, and shaving later I finally feel human again.

I slip into a red wine lace bra, matching panties, and a short crushed velvet wrap dress. I smile at my reflection as I imagine Brooks' reaction when he sees what I'm wearing underneath. He's like a bull seeing red when I wear lingerie. This week alone he destroyed two pairs of panties and one of my less sturdy bras. I'm going to have to hit Sally up for some new panties soon if he keeps it up.

The hotel room smells like heaven when I come out, still towel-drying my hair. Brooks is dressed (such a shame) in jeans and a gray sweater, but his feet are bare as he sits at the little dining table. A table piled with breakfast food. It looks like he ordered one of everything off the room service menu.

"Oh sweet baby Jesus, thank you!" I hadn't realized how hungry I was but now my stomach is growling, demanding one of those waffles with lots of maple syrup. And bacon. Definitely bacon.

Brooks pulls out a chair for me, kissing my neck as I sit. He lifts the warming cloche sitting on top of the plate in front of me, but instead of food there is a small robin's egg blue box tied with a white satin ribbon.

"Merry Christmas," Brooks says as he sits down in the chair next to mine and makes a little go on gesture. He's wearing a huge smile. The smile he only ever gives to me.

"I feel bad though! Your present is at my gran's house. I thought we were opening presents there later, so I didn't bring it."

He gives me a sweeping, predatory gaze that makes me instantly wet. "Just let me unwrap that dress later and see what you're wearing underneath. That's all I want for Christmas."

"Keep looking at me and talking to me like that and I'll have to get fresh panties," I mutter under my breath trying to ignore the furious blush in my cheeks.

He chuckles darkly. "How long is Christmas Day with your family?"

"Too long," I groan as I untie the white ribbon and remove the little lid. Inside the box is a gold necklace with a tiny branch of leaves. "It's beautiful," I sigh as I trace a finger along the leaves.

"It's an olive branch." Brooks grins as he leans forward, taking the box from my hands and removing the necklace. He stands again, fastening it around my neck.

For a second, I think I'm going to cry. No one has ever given me a gift like this. "That's fitting, given the way we started out," I laugh softly. "Thank you. I love it," I tell him as I lean back for a kiss. Brooks' fingers trace over the necklace where it rests just below my collarbone, sending a little shiver down my spine.

"I thought you might," he says as he settles into his chair next to mine, a satisfied grin on his face. "I wanted you to have something you could wear to remind you of how I feel about you." I had been looking down at my necklace, admiring the delicate olive leaves, but my eyes jump back to his face.

"How do you feel about me?" I whisper.

He takes my hand, kissing the backs of my fingers while his stormy eyes track my face with an intensity I've never seen from anyone else. Sometimes when he looks at me like that I swear he can see right through to my soul.

His eyes crinkle with a hint of a smile. "I'm in love with you, Olive. I love everything about you."

His smile has turned vulnerable, like he's afraid I'm going to tell him to hit the road. I can't help tearing up this time. My whole life, I never thought I'd find someone like Brooks. Hell, I never thought I'd be able to even let someone close enough to love me, let alone love them in return. But I do. I love him and trust him with all my heart.

"I love you too," I say, blinking back tears. Reaching out to touch his cheek, I try to memorize the look on his face and the feeling of his soft scruffy beard under my fingers. I've never seen him smile so hard. I'm so full of joy that I feel like a balloon about to burst. Can being too happy make someone explode? Because I just might.

Brooks kisses me, cradling my jaw in his work-roughened hands. He kisses me like I'm all he will ever want and I kiss him back, knowing that he is it for me. I'll spend the rest of my life with him and die a happy, well-loved woman.

He kisses me until I lose all track of time, but there's an annoying buzzing in the background and I finally realize it's my stupid phone. I wonder if I can chuck it out the hotel window and curl up in bed with Brooks for the rest of eternity.

The buzzing stops, and immediately starts up again. Groaning, Brooks grabs my phone and checks the caller ID.

"It's Julia," he sighs heavily before handing it over.

It stops vibrating and for one glorious second I think maybe she won't call again. But of course she does. My phone lights up with her name, and I have no choice but to answer.

"Bad timing, Jul--" I start but she interrupts me.

"It's Christmas. Everyone is here except for you and if you don't hurry up Gran is going to kick your ass."

"Pfft. I'd like to see her try," I huff.

Someone says something in the background, I think it's Lilah, but it's hard to tell. "If you hurry up, we promise to keep Gran from petting Brooks," Julia promises with a laugh.

Brooks must be able to hear her side of the call because he stands up and yells, "Deal," before grabbing our bags and throwing stuff inside haphazardly. Julia laughs as I hang up on her.

"But breakfast…" Am I whining? Maybe a little, but I'm starving and there's a veritable mountain of food untouched on the table.

Brooks quickly wraps an arm around my waist and kisses me before releasing me and going to the hotel phone. He punches in a number and asks them to bring up takeout boxes before giving me a wolfish grin. "You eat," he says. "I'll finish packing and we can bring the leftovers to share. If it means I won't get felt up by your grandmother, I can skip breakfast."

Chapter 41: Brooks

True to their word, Olive's sisters run interference when we get to her childhood home. Gran hugs me around the middle and just as she starts feeling up my bicep, Lilah pops her head out of another room.

"Gran, do you smell something burning?"

"Oh shit, my gingerbread!" Gran yells before hustling off towards the kitchen, straightening her "Drink Up, Grinches" apron. Lilah shoots Olive a wink, making her laugh.

Christmas with Olive's family is so different from the quiet, restrained holidays I grew up with. Maybe it's because I was an only child, but my parents never seemed to get in the holiday spirit. Decorating was "unnecessary" and "a waste of time."

It's clear Olive's grandmother does not share that opinion. Lights are strung from every tree in the front and back yards of the house. In the house, Gran has three full size Christmas trees decorated in different themes and a Christmas village so big that Asher built a mantel extension to display all of it. The whole house feels packed with cheerful people, music, and amazing smells.

I'm not ashamed to admit that I'm selfish with Olive, keeping her close as much as possible. I pull her into my lap under the guise of making room on the couch for everyone else. She rolls her eyes but wiggles back on my lap, smiling knowingly when I can't control the way I harden under her.

She knows I'm dying to get back inside her. I wish her family could have given us at least another hour alone, but it's Christmas and this is what their family does. It's worth the blue balls to make her happy and spend the day with her tucked up into my lap.

Olive's family exchanges gifts, trading each other boxes containing a real gift and a gag gift. "It's something Grandpa always did," Olive explains.

Asher hands me a box while wearing a pair of mittens with googly eyes sewn onto the knuckles. "This is from all of us," he says with a straight face.

Inside is a really nice bottle of bourbon and… "Is that a Karate Kid chia pet?" I ask.

"YUP!" Lukas calls out from across the living room while Olive laughs, trying not to spew her mouthful of hot cocoa.

"Where did you guys even find that?" She asks.

Lukas shrugs. "Amazon."

"Thanks," I smile at each of them. "I'm not sure where I'll put the chia pet. Maybe poolside?" I ask Olive. She grins and I can't help imagining how sexy she's going to look swimming in the pool this spring.

"Open mine," Olive says while crawling under the tree to pull out a large flat box from the back. The wrapping paper has reindeer wearing sunglasses and they're throwing the cloven hoof version of gang signs.

Laughing at the wrapping paper, I tear into it and lift the lid of the box. Inside is a star chart framed with the words, The Night We Met. Olive looks up at me through her lashes. "It's the night sky over Napa on the night we met."

"I fucking love it," I tell her as I pull her back into my lap for a kiss.

"Oh thank god!" She laughs against my lips. "Look underneath it." She points back at the box and wiggles like an excited puppy, stirring up sensations I'd rather not have in front of her entire family.

Lifting the large frame out of the box reveals a layer of Styrofoam peanuts below. I swipe my hand through it and come up with a CD case.

"Oh Jesus. Bon Jovi's Greatest Hits?" I ask her with a grin. Olive laughs so hard she almost topples off my lap, but I catch her. Julia cackles, and Lilah tries to hide her laugh behind her hand.

"What's so funny about Bon Jovi?" Lukas asks. Asher shrugs. It seems the brothers haven't been given the details of how we met, which is probably lucky for me. I may be big, but there are two of them.

"Nothing," Olive replies. "It was just playing the night we met."

She throws her arms around my neck and snuggles into me. Breathing her in, I take a minute to be thankful for the way she feels in my arms; the soft vanilla scent of her body pressed against mine and the way she's fearlessly let me into her heart.

"Thank you, baby," I tell her as I stroke her hair.

After gifts, we sit and chat in the living room, drinking cocoa while Christmas movies play in the background. There's a knock on the front door and before anyone can get up, Luis pops his head inside.

"Knock knock! Look who I brought!" I don't miss the way Julia's head whips up or the disappointment that crumples her face when she sees the man that follows Luis inside. Olive doesn't miss it either, and she stands up looking torn between being polite to Luis and comforting her sister. I give her a gentle push towards Julia while I stand to shake Luis' hand, blocking them from view.

"Mateo!" Gran cries as she wraps the man in a bear hug before patting his cheeks. "Look how handsome you've gotten!"

Luis beams with pride as he introduces me to his younger son, Mateo. "He got shore leave for Christmas and surprised me this morning!" I've never seen Luis smile so hard.

Mateo shakes my hand. He's got to be ten years my junior with an innocent, clean shaven look, fitting his navy uniform. "I've heard you're dating Olive," he says with a grin as Olive and her siblings pile in around us, hugging him all at once. My girl seems to have gotten Julia put back together because she's joined in the fray.

Olive pulls back and tilts her head to the side with a soft, sweet smile, all for me. She doesn't take her eyes off me while she answers him. "Yeah, we're dating."

Her look warms me all the way through and I raise a corner of my mouth, returning her smile. She makes me so damn happy.

Chapter 42: Olive

With the addition of Mateo and Luis to the party, the living room is filled to capacity. Gran has dozens of cookies already baked for us and, for once, I don't cook or bake anything at all. I'm content sitting on Brooks' lap while we all catch up.

Mateo keeps everyone entertained with stories of his ship mates. Luis' younger son was like a brother to us, growing up. You'd never know it now, but he was a troublemaking pipsqueak when we were young. Six years younger than me, Asher, and his big brother Javier, he was an adorable menace, trailing after us with an eye out for mischief. He joined the Navy straight out of high school and we haven't seen much of him since. It's nice to have him here.

Having Mateo and Luis here makes this feel like the holidays of my childhood. We are missing Javier, of course. Asher's best friend can't get away from work in New York, but no one expected him to.

Poor Julia was so hopeful Javier had come home when Luis popped in to surprise us. She always had a soft spot for Javier, following us around as kids. As a teenager she hid it well, but internally swooned whenever he was around. I always hoped he would notice her; I even tried to nudge him in her direction a time or two, but it never seemed to take.

When he left for NYU with a full-ride soccer scholarship, she hid in her room for weeks, only coming alive when he came home for a visit, mourning each time he left. I wish there were someone else for her. Nursing makes her happy, but it's not the same as love.

I thought I was complete before I met Brooks. That I didn't need anything or anyone else. I had my family and my career. And it's true, I was content; I wasn't unhappy. But now, I understand it was like a piece of my soul was lost, wandering the universe, trying to get back to me. It was a piece I'd never had, so how could I know that it was missing? I couldn't feel the loss until Brooks put it back in place, mending my soul and making me whole.

I want that for my brothers and sisters. I want to see each of them made whole, too. I see now that the damage of our childhood doesn't make us unlovable. It doesn't have to prevent us from choosing to love and trust.

I make a silent vow that, if given the opportunity, I'll encourage my siblings to find the same kind of happiness I've found. I might have to push them the way Lilah pushed me. Or, more accurately, the way she set things in motion with startling insight. Remembering the way she screamed and dodged Chelsea's bouquet last night, I think she might be a bit of a challenge.

Last night. Oh lord. Last night was amazing. Wrong time and place to have a wandering mind, but I can't help the replay of Christmas Eve. The way he tossed me on the bed like I weighed nothing. The love bites on my inner thighs, still visible this morning. I wonder if they're still there and I press my thighs together at the thought.

'Oh fuck. You're so wet. Did you get yourself all worked up teasing me?' Brooks' voice echoes in my mind. Talking dirty is officially my catnip. I'm pretty sure I'd give him anything he wanted if he asked for it in that bedroom voice of his. 'Jesus Christ, that's fucking sexy. Look at that ass bounce while I fuck you.'

Just the thought of him gripping my hips while he fucked me from behind has me squirming in his lap. I'm trying to hold still, to block it out of my mind. Wrong time, wrong place, I chastise myself. It doesn't matter what I try to tell my vagina, though; she is not listening.

Chapter 43: Brooks

I'm absentmindedly rubbing little circles against Olive's hip when I notice her shifting and pressing her thighs together.

"You ok, baby girl?" I whisper in her ear.

"Yup," she smiles; but there's no missing the lust in her eyes.

"What are you thinking about?" I ask quietly, as she rubs her thighs together again. It's so slight I don't think anyone else could even see it, but I can feel the way she's tensing and squirming in my lap. She's turned on by whatever she's got going on in her head right now, and I'm dying to know what it is.

She pauses and for a second I think she's not going to answer me but then she leans into me, her lips brush the sensitive skin of my ear, setting my blood to boiling as she whispers very quietly, "Last night. The way you talked dirty while you fucked me."

Oh god damn. It takes everything in me not to groan out loud and haul her ass to the nearest dark room with a lock. Seeing as that might be inappropriate given the present company, I opt for subtlety instead.

"Can you give me the tour? I need to use the restroom and I'd like to see your old room," I say, lifting her off my lap and setting her on her feet in front of me. That's about as subtle as I get.

"Of course." She smiles, but there's a flash of warning and heat in her eyes. I grin back, trying not to look as predatory as I feel.

I follow her swaying ass down the hall and up the stairs. As she climbs them ahead of me, I can see little glimpses of her red lace panties riding high on her ass cheeks and the shadow where they tuck into the perfect cleft of her backside.

At the top of the stairs she turns left and walks to the end of the hallway before opening a door and stepping inside. It's a generic guest room, nothing left of Olive to interest me, but I follow her in.

"This was the room I shared with Lilah. It's the guest room now--"

I cut her off, gently pressing my hand over her mouth while quietly closing the door with my other hand.

"Don't make a sound or everyone will know what we're up to," I whisper as I lay my palm on her stomach, loving the way she feels under my hand. Her eyes light up as she realizes what I'm saying. Mischief curls her lips into a smile under my fingers as I walk her back against the wall and pin her there with my body. "Are you going to be a good girl and stay quiet?"

She nods, her breaths come in excited little huffs through her nose and she's watching me with burning fascination. The little flecks of gold in her iris seem to glow even as her pupils dilate.

"Did you think I wouldn't notice how turned on you were? Wriggling your sexy ass in my lap like that. I see everything about you, Olive. You're my whole world and I'm going to make sure you have exactly what you need, no matter who is nearby."

Sliding my palm down her belly, I run my fingertips down her leg and back up her inner thigh, sliding right under her dress. I'm not wasting time. I'd bet we have five minutes before someone starts to wonder where we snuck off to.

I yank her panties down, letting them fall to the floor as I press my knee between her thighs, using my leg to spread hers. Slipping a finger into her pussy, I groan quietly at the drenching heat. "Holy fuck, you're so wet." She moans into my hand.

"Shhh, baby," I tell her before releasing her mouth. Removing my finger from her warmth, I put it to her lips. "Suck it," I demand. "See how good you taste." I almost come when she takes my finger into her mouth, eyeing me darkly and giving it a strong suck before releasing it with a little pop.

"Good girl," I whisper as I cover her mouth with my hand again and thrust my finger back into her pussy. I keep her pressed tight to the wall with my body, letting her feel the size of me and how much she turns me on. "Is this what you need?" I whisper gruffly in her ear, adding another finger and using them to fuck her hard.

Her sweet vanilla scent mixed with the musk of her arousal has me dying to pop her on my cock and let her bounce there, pinned between me and the wall, but there's no time. The risk of getting caught might be hot, but the idea of her grandmother or a brother walking in and catching me balls deep in my woman is not. I just need to see her come. Need to take the edge off for her.

"Does this greedy little pussy need to be filled?" She moans into my palm, legs shaking as I double down my assault on her g-spot.

"Shh, shh, shh," I whisper, rubbing my palm into her clit. "Don't want everyone to know what a dirty girl you are for me. You're all mine and so is this pussy." Her eyes are shut and her body is writhing against the wall, desperate for release.

"Look at me so I know you understand," I growl. She opens her eyes, hooded with lust. "Good girl," I tell her again. "You're mine. This pussy is mine and you're going to come for me, Olive."

It's a damn good thing I'm covering her mouth because she comes like a hurricane, wailing into my hand as she convulses and shakes. I have to use my body to hold her up against the wall, or she would collapse. When she finally settles and regains her balance, I grab a tissue from the bedside table and clean her up before pulling her panties back into place.

She laughs shakily. "Wow… that was… so dirty. I love you."

Grinning back at her, I've never been happier. "I love you too. Merry Christmas."

Chapter 44: Olive

Three Months Later...

Looking through the window at what used to be part of my parking lot, I admire the finest ass to ever be wrapped in denim. Brooks took the day off so he could sit in on my first class in the new addition. He's currently wandering around in there looking for any faults. We both know he won't find any. The addition passed every inspection with flying colors but that doesn't stop him from being a perfectionist.

I'm beyond excited about this first class: Buttercream Basics. I have everything prepped and recipe packets printed for each attendee, even though it's almost entirely filled with friends and family. They all wanted to be here to support me, so I can't complain.

I've got two more classes scheduled in March: French Macarons for Beginners, and Eclairs and Cream Puffs. They both sold out within two days of posting them on my website. Lilah and I have been staying up late putting together more class ideas. We even have a Girl's Night Out planned, featuring dessert tastings and cocktails with dirty names, a la Chelsea's bachelorette party.

A few hours later, I'm standing in the front of my classroom doing a demo on how to use a turntable to buttercream a cake as twenty people follow along at their stations. My brothers are more interested in eating the frosting than covering a cake, but at least Julia and our grandmother are focused. Julia is concentrating so hard that her tongue is sticking out the side of her mouth.

Leaving my station at the front of the room, I walk around, giving everyone pointers and smacking Lukas' hand as he tries to steal another finger of buttercream from his bowl. Lilah is following me around, snapping photos for the website. I hope she caught that on film. I'm going to frame it and give it to him for Christmas next year.

When I get to Brooks, I can see he's struggling. The man can spackle walls, paint, and use a nail gun like a badass, but buttercream just isn't his forte. I correct the way he's holding the offset spatula and realize his hands are shaking slightly.

"Are you ok?" I ask him as I take his hand. I'm worried about him. I mean, I've never seen him so much as tremble. He squeezes my hand in his much larger one and seems to settle a little.

"Yeah, just nervous," he answers me with a smile.

"Oh, well, that's to be expected. I'm very intimidating," I joke, letting out a laugh as I stroke his bicep.

"It's not that. I just want to get this right," he says. I give him a quizzical look as he sets the spatula down and reaches into his pocket and pulls out a little box.

"Oh my god," I whisper. "What are you doing?" My heartbeat pounds in my ears so hard I almost miss his response.

"I'm making you mine forever." Brooks drops to one knee right in the middle of the classroom. His dark blue eyes are piercing, but his mouth turns up in a small smile as he opens the box and holds out an obscenely enormous diamond solitaire ring.

The room spins around me as I try to stop the excited ringing and thumping in my ears. This is happening. This is really fucking happening. The rest of the world dissolves away, leaving just the two of us.

"From the first moment I saw you, I wanted you more than I've ever wanted anything in my life. Every day with you is better than the last and I wake up so grateful that you chose to let me in. That you put your trust in me. I want to spend the rest of my life waking up with that feeling. I want to spend the rest of my life loving you and having you love me in return."

Brooks takes a steadying breath, his smile crinkling the little lines around his eyes the way that I love so, so much.

"Olive, will you marry me?"

"Holy fuck." I'm so lost in Brooks that I didn't even realize it was me whispering it until everyone starts laughing. "Yes! Oh my god, yes! I love you!" I shout.

Brooks launches to his feet, swinging me off mine. He holds me tight, kissing me like he'll never let me go. I hug him close, knowing deep in my heart that he won't back away. He won't leave me. He won't stop wanting me. He'll always love me as much as I love him.

Epilogue - Olive

S hot! Shot! Shot! WOOOOOO!"

I grimace as I choke back the tequila shot and sour lime wedge chaser. Yikes. Tequila is really Julia's thing, but I'm playing along. I don't want to be a stick-in-the-mud tonight, especially considering that this Girl's Night Out is being held in honor of my engagement.

Sally, Lilah, Julia, and Chelsea coordinated my kidnapping from work. They even confiscated my phone, texting Brooks to tell him they would bring me home safe… and a little drunk.

Lilah slides onto the barstool next to me wearing a short red dress and a big smile. She hugs me, slightly unsteady thanks to our last round of shots, and grabs my hand, inspecting my ring.

"Are you sure he's actually human?" she asks with a grin. "He's almost too perfect for you."

"He is, isn't he? I got crazy lucky, I guess," I say, stroking a fingertip over the magnificent ring he put on my finger last week. My cheeks hurt from smiling so much. "Are you all unpacked? How is home ownership going?" I ask.

Lilah avoids eye contact, a sure sign that she's keeping something from me. "It's great. It would be better if my neighbor didn't have to mow his damn lawn every Saturday at 8am."

Cocking my head to the side, I wiggle my eyebrows at her. "Is this the nerdy guy with the Texas accent?"

She smacks me on the shoulder with a slight laugh. "He's not nerdy! Or maybe he is. I don't know. But you can't call someone nerdy just because they wear glasses. He's too handsome to be called a nerd anyway," she sighs an alcohol-laden breath.

"Oh yeah?" I ask. "How handsome?" I really shouldn't take advantage of my sister being tipsy to dig for info, but she's been so determined to hate the early-morning mower until now. Suddenly she's all wistful sighs and I'm a nosy bitch so I can't help myself. Chelsea, Sally and Julia have been tearing it up behind us, dancing wildly in the space they cleared of tables and chairs but it looks like it's time to move to the next bar because Sally is circling her finger in the air in the universal signal for "Let's move."

Lilah, oblivious to all of their shenanigans, plunks her head down on the bar and moans, "He's annoyingly handsome. It's like someone rolled up all the sexiest bits of Henry Cavill and Dierks Bentley."

"Well, that begs the question, Bentley in 2004 or 2020, and Henry Cavill in The Witcher or Henry Cavill in The Tudors?" I ask as Sally herds us off our bar stools and out onto the sidewalk.

Lilah laughs roughly and gives a full body shiver. "Henry Cavill circa Batman vs. Superman and Bentley... well all the time with the damn voice."

"Mother of god, you've got the weirdest taste in men," I laugh as we step out onto the street. The streetlights are all lit up, illuminating people walking down First Street. It finally feels like spring, the air warm and smelling like rain.

We only make it a couple of feet down the sidewalk before a big black SUV pulls into a driveway blocking our path. "Jesus! Watch it!" I yell. I'm interrupted by the driver's door opening and I start to panic. Crap on a cracker. I hope I didn't incite some crazy ass road rage just now.

A man's foot hits the ground and I'm ready to rip my heels off, already debating whether to try to run away barefoot or hit him with my shoes, when Chelsea starts laughing.

"What took you so long?" she asks the man as he steps out of the shadow of the car door. She points at her watch. "It took you almost an hour to come find me. I feel like you're slipping."

"I knew you were having fun," he says with a chuckle.

"Matt?" I start to ask why he's crashing girl's night but a split-second later Brooks comes around from the passenger side, stalking towards me with a dark and possessive look on his face. Ooh. Yes, please! My inner bad girl does a little dance. Without saying a word, he tosses me over his shoulder.

"Who's got her phone?" he demands. I can't see what's going on, just a solid view of my fiancé's backside. I can't say I'm complaining.

Upside down or not, I can hear just fine. "I've got it," says Julia with an exasperated laugh. "You could have let us have her for one night, you know. Here, take it."

I hear the sound of something slapping into a hand as Brooks grumbles. "You turned her phone off. How am I supposed to relax when I have no idea where you took her? Besides, I had plans for her tonight."

I'm jostled as he tucks my phone in his pocket and heads back to the SUV.

"Ok, ew!" Julia calls out after us. I laugh as I use his lower back to push myself up and wave at them.

"Thanks for the girl's night!" I call back. "Next time we turn off all the phones."

Brooks growls underneath me like a pissed off bear. He deposits me in the passenger seat, reaching over me to do the seatbelt. Looking back at my sisters and friends, I see Matt has an arm around Chelsea and they're all heading off down the street.

"Are we just stealing Matt's car now?"

"He's got a driver on standby. He'll make sure everyone else gets home safe," Brooks says. His voice is surprisingly gentle. "I should feel bad for kidnapping you but I don't." His words are defiant but the look on his face is resigned, like he's just waiting for me to tell him off.

Slipping my arms around his neck, I purr, "The girls and I, we had our fun. I'm ready to go home with you now. Besides, you said you had plans for me?"

Brooks cocks an eyebrow and the corner of his mouth lifts in that way it only does for me. "Yes, ma'am I do. I've got plans for you every day for the rest of our lives."

Epilogue - Brooks

Three days. It's been exactly 72 hours since Olive and I said 'I do.' The best 72 hours of my life.

Walking out of the ocean after my swim, I find my exhausted wife dozing under an umbrella on the sun deck of our beach house. Her golden skin glows in the late afternoon sun and the curtains behind her flap in the breeze. It's a damn good thing we have this whole stretch of beach to ourselves because she's wearing a little white bikini and she might as well wave a red flag in front of a bull. I'd be out of my damn mind if there was anyone close enough to see my wife like this. Grinning at her sleeping form, I pad towards her. She does this on purpose. She knows I can't keep my hands off her when she looks like that. Shit, I can't keep my hands off no matter what. I'll take her un-showered and wearing my old sweat pants. In fact, sometimes I prefer it.

I strip off my swim trunks and crawl over her on the oversized chaise. Salt water drips off me and beads on her stomach, drawing up little goosebumps on her skin. The scent of her coconut sunscreen mixing with the vanilla of her skin is almost more than I can bear as I carefully pull her bikini top aside.

The breeze kicks up, making her dusky pink nipple tighten right in front of me. I groan as I draw the tight bud into my mouth, cupping her other breast and settling my hips on top of hers. I need her. I need her right now and I can't wait for her to finish her nap. I've had her more times than I can count since we got married, but I'm still achingly hard.

Olive wakes with a little moan, arching into me. "That wasn't much of a nap, you know." It would sound like a complaint if she didn't sound so breathy and wasn't lifting her hips to grind her pussy against the hard length of my dick.

"I'm sorry," I tell her, even though I'm definitely not sorry. "I can go back inside and let you sleep." I feign lifting myself off her but she grabs me by the shoulders, suddenly very awake.

"Don't you fucking dare," she growls. Chuckling, I move my mouth to her other breast, licking and biting her nipple until she's panting and moaning underneath me.

I yank her bottoms to the side, too impatient to be inside her again to untie anything. With one hard thrust I bury myself, filling her wet pussy, growling into her throat as she gasps.

"Fuck. You. Feel. So. Good," I grind out each word as I piston into her, reveling in the way her fingernails bite into my biceps. She arches and lifts her hips to meet my thrusts, as desperate as I am.

I sit back on my knees, gripping her hips and jacking her on my dick furiously. She comes, screaming and clenching around my punishing thrusts, crying out my name. The tight aching in my balls finally eases as I come, emptying myself deep inside my wife with shuddering pleasure.

Rolling off her, I slide her bikini back into place before pulling her onto my chest. She cuddles into me like a trusting little kitten.

"I love you," I tell her as I run my fingers up and down her back.

"I love you more," she yawns, wrapping her arm around my middle and squeezing me before falling back asleep. I fight back the urge to nod off right away, content to stroke her skin and soak up as much of this feeling as I can.

The End.

Coming Soon: Mowed Over
by Mae Harden

Lilah

"NO! No no no no no! Why?!" I yell as I fling the covers off. My intention is to stomp through my little bungalow, rip the front door open and confront my jackass early bird of a neighbor.

Instead, my feet tangle in the top sheet and I fall out of bed, smacking my face on the end table. That's just great. Add a head wound on top of exhaustion. I manage to stumble to my feet and make it to my front door, propelled mostly by rage.

"How many times?" I mutter to myself as I throw open the door. "How many times have I asked him nicely not to mow at 8am?"

"Benjamin!" I yell as I stomp across my overgrown lawn. I know I'm not dressed to be outside. The tank top and shorts I was sleeping in are threadbare but I sure as shit don't care right now. "You promised! You fucking swore you wouldn't do this again!"

He can't hear me, of course. His mower is running at a million decibels and his big, stupid, muscled back is still turned. I studiously ignore the way those back muscles ripple as he pushes along. That sweat dripping down his thick arms? Not distracting at all. I won't even acknowledge how those low-slung athletic shorts cling to his glorious ass and thighs. Nope. None of it.

I make it to the edge of my property and huff, standing barefoot with my hands on my hips. Ben is just turning his mower back when he sees me. His eyes widen and he kills the mower just as I yell his name at the top of my lungs again. Do I sound bitchy? Probably. But Ben doesn't seem to mind. His face brightens and his mouth pulls up at one corner in the beginnings of a smirk. He's sporting a short beard along his jaw. Well something between a 5 o'clock shadow and a beard. Whatever you call it, it's sexy as hell. He has a white t-shirt tossed over one shoulder, and he uses it to wipe the sweat from his brow as he walks towards me. He straightens his black-framed glasses and I die a little. I love a man with glasses. He doesn't wear them all the time but he should.

"Sorry Lilah, I didn't think you were home..." he trails off as he looks at my face. "Jesus, what happened?" Ben reaches out to touch my forehead.

"YOU happened, Benjamin!" I snap back. ""You and that stupid lawn-- Ow!" His fingers graze the bump where my head connected with my end table, and they come away with blood. I've been running on anger and adrenaline since I was so rudely awoken but the sight of the blood on his fingers, my blood, and the concern on Ben's face is enough to tamp down my rage. My hand flies up to my head, and I touch the huge lump with dawning horror. That's kind of a lot of blood.

"Lilah, do you have a first aid kit?" Ben asks me, brow furrowed.

"I think I have some bandaids," I reply shakily. I honestly couldn't be sure if I even have those, though. If I do, they are probably still in a box somewhere. I moved in two months ago, but I've been so busy that unpacking has been unbearably slow. I work at the bar almost every night until 3am and then help my sister at her bakery most days, too. I'm rarely home unless I'm trying to get some sleep.

Unpacking just hasn't seemed that important until now. But the thought of Benjamin walking into my house has me a little panicked. There are boxes piled up in the corners of every room, and I know for a fact that I have at least six bras and a dozen panties hanging on a drying rack in my living room. At least my bathroom is clean. I've got that going for me, I guess.

"How do you not have a first aid kit? You're a grown ass woman, right?" Ben teases.

"I just moved in, jackass," I reply sarcastically. He's still smiling at me like it's adorable that I swore at him.

"Well come on," he says as he takes my elbow and starts leading me toward his house. Part of me wants to pull my arm free and the other part of me loves the possessive grip. His hand is huge, a little calloused, and so warm on my skin. He's not being overly rough with me but he's not particularly gentle, either. A delicious little shiver goes through me as Ben snaps his gaze towards me and tilts his head in a look that I can't decipher.

"You're not a serial killer, right? Like you're not planning on handcuffing me in your basement or anything?" I say it as a joke, but the second I do, my paranoid side reminds me that it is really stupid to go into some guy's house when I barely know him. He's just being nice, I remind myself. This is why I need to stop listening to true crime podcasts.

Ben raises an eyebrow. "Not without your consent," he replies.

I bark out a laugh. It's not a very ladylike sound, but most of our conversations have consisted of me begging him not to do loud yard work first thing in the morning, and yelling at him when he does it anyway. I've never heard him joke before. Joke or not, the thought of him tying me to his bed and fucking me senseless has a certain appeal. Not that I would EVER admit that.

"Well, consent not given. At least not today."

Ben quirks an eyebrow up at me. "Bondage not your thing?" he asks. I can feel my face flush. I'm suddenly very aware that my hand is still in his.

"I wouldn't know," I squeak. My cheeks are burning and I'd bet anything I look like a tomato right now.

Ben leads me through the front door into his home. The living room is tasteful, with matching brown leather couches and a chaise. There's actual art on the walls. Photographs, I realize. Everything is warm and comfortable and feels... expensive? His bungalow is the mirror image of mine and it's surreal to walk into a home that's so similar and yet feels so different. My house still feels unsettled and a little lonely when I come home. I'm proud of it and I love it but it's a work in progress and doesn't have the lived-in coziness of Ben's home.

"Sit," Ben says with a crooked smile. "Stay."

I glare at him as he chuckles and walks towards the back of the house, disappearing behind the bedroom door. He reemerges a minute later carrying an overly large red first aid bag. Maybe it's the wrong moment to notice the way he walks; but his long, masculine stride is incredibly sexy.

Ben sets the bag on the coffee table before pulling it closer. When he sits next to me on the couch, his thigh presses against mine and his closeness is alarming. I should scoot away, I know, but... I don't want to. Instead, I angle my body so that I'm facing him, our bare knees touching.

I would have thought he would put a shirt on when he disappeared to get the bag, but his tan skin is still glistening and bare. Sitting this close I can see the dusting of light brown hair on his chest and the sheen of sweat that really shouldn't be sexy. Not sexy at all... I suddenly realize I'm staring and my eyes shoot up to meet his. I must have a really guilty look on my face because Ben looks smug as hell.

"Shit. Sorry," I mutter.

"Why?" Ben asks, amusement in his voice. "Look all you want. I don't mind." He's still chuckling as he starts pulling little packets, gauze, and tape out of his bag. He puts on a pair of gloves and opens an antibacterial cleansing cloth. "Look, this is going to sting, but you need to hold still." I nod as he leans in even closer and touches it to my forehead. It does sting a bit as he gently wipes my forehead clean of blood, but I don't care. His face is inches from mine and sweet baby Jesus, I can smell him. He smells like fresh soap and sweat and when he breathes his breath is vaguely minty.

Oh god! I'm hit with a horrible realization. I scrambled out of bed to yell at him. I didn't shower or brush my teeth, I didn't even look in a mirror. How shitty is my hair?! I must smell awful. My eyes must have gone wide because Ben pulls his head back a bit to look at my face as he works on me.

"Are you ok? Does that hurt?" he asks.

"Oh, no. I mean, yes a little but it doesn't bother me." I reply. "I mean, I have a high pain tolerance. I'm not going to be a baby about a little antiseptic." He smiles at me as I babble. His eyes have that calculating intensity again but they never lose the sweet looking crinkles at the corners. I snap my mouth shut and resist the urge to fix my hair. I don't think I even want to know how bad it is.

Ben squeezes antibiotic ointment onto a q-tip and then his big hand is cupping my jaw, holding me still while he spreads the ointment to my forehead. I watch his eyes as he focuses on his work. This feels incredibly intimate. I'm almost disappointed when he lets my face go, but I hold still and let him tape a large square of gauze over my injury.

"There. No more gaping head wound." He sits back with a smile and cracks a disposable ice pack and puts it on my forehead. "Hold that there for 15 minutes." He starts to clean up all the trash from fixing me up. As he gets up he says, "Tell me again how all of this was my fault."